Why not?

BOOK ONE

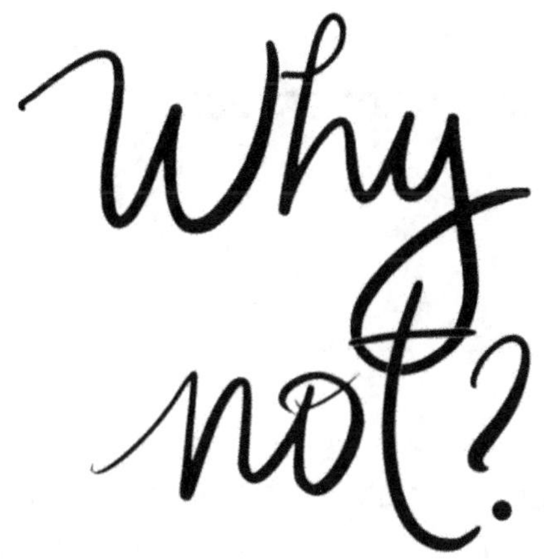

SABRINE SADLER

BOOK ONE

Legal deposit - Bibliothèque et Archives nationales du Québec, 2025.

ISBN 978-2-9818559-0-9 (paperback edition)

Book design by Isabelle Rocheleau

WHATEVER YOU THINK YOU CAN
DO, OR DREAM YOU CAN, BEGIN IT.
BOLDNESS HAS GENIUS, POWER AND
MAGIC IN IT.

-GOETHE

One

"The usual?" the waiter asked, a knowing smile playing on his lips.

Talie nodded absently, her thoughts drifting. *I'll never understand why regulars take such pride in being served without saying a word. It's not even flattering. How did I end up in this ridiculous situation?*

"Hey, girl! Been here long?" Rebecca's voice cut through the noise, pulling Talie back to reality.

"Only about ten minutes. Are you alone? I thought the girls from the agency were coming," she replied, brushing a strand of hair behind her ear.

Rebecca shrugged with casual indifference. "No, they changed their minds."

"How surprising," she said, her tone dripping with sarcasm as her friend's gaze swept over her, taking in the fitted clothes she wore.

"You got all dressed up for Jesse?" Rebecca teased. "New bra too, I bet."

"You know me."

"Shopping addict! If you keep it up, you'll need a whole room just for lingerie."

"Everyone's got their vice," Talie replied with a smirk.

Rebecca leaned closer, her voice dropping to a whisper. "If only someone appreciated it properly…"

Talie grimaced, brushing off the comment as she scanned the room. Her gaze darted from one corner to another, a restless search for Jesse amid the sea of faces. The club was alive with energy, its rhythm syncing with the quickening beat of her heart.

"Has Jesse come to see you?" Rebecca asked, tossing her blonde hair over her shoulder.

A flicker of desperation crossed her voice, so faint it was almost imperceptible. "Not yet."

The waiter returned, setting a martini on the table. "Lychee martini for the lady," he said as Talie handed him the money.

"And one for you?" he added, his gaze lingering a beat too long on Rebecca's cleavage.

"Why not?" she purred, her lips curving into a broad, suggestive grin. As he walked away, her eyes followed him like a predator tracking its prey. "I wouldn't mind some… alone time with him."

"You're hopeless."

"Why?" she asked, her voice light, feigning innocence.

"Come on! It's pathetic that we're spending more time here with these strangers than with our families."

"It's just a hobby, a way to relax. Like going to the movies or the theater."

"A hobby! Seriously? Am I getting too old for this?"

"Stop worrying about your age!"

"Look at us—thirty, single, and wasting our nights in a ladies' night club. Kind of depressing."

Rebecca tilted her head, studying her friend. "You don't like coming here anymore?"

Weary of the monotony that clouded her days, Talie let out a sigh, her gaze wandering aimlessly until Jesse finally appeared. He was more magnetic than ever, his chiseled frame exuding a commanding sensuality that seemed to ripple with each step. Under the soft, shifting lights, his tanned skin gleamed, carrying a hint of something rugged, almost intoxicating. As he strode toward the stage, he ran a hand through his tousled blonde hair, the movement slow and deliberate, as if he knew the effect it had on every pair of eyes in the room. Then his piercing blue gaze found hers, locking on with an intensity that stripped away the noise of the world, leaving only the rapid beat of her heart and the charged air between them.

"Ladies!" the host announced, drawing out the words in a sultry tone. "Please welcome Jesse the Seducer."

The music exploded through the speakers, and Jesse leaped onto the stage, his every move dripping with raw, seductive energy that seemed to electrify the room. Talie's breath caught in her throat, her heart pounding wildly as a whirlwind of emotions surged within her.

"You don't want to come anymore?" Rebecca repeated, smirking at her friend's transfixed expression.

"I'm completely lost," she murmured, voice barely above a whisper, eyes fixed on Jesse.

"He's all yours now. Indulge yourself."

Talie went quiet, her focus solely on him as he twirled, jumped, and removed pieces of clothing. Women screamed his name, teasing him with dollar bills held between their lips—bills he eagerly took with quick, stolen kisses. Club Viator's dancers were known as the sexiest in town, but Jesse held the title of the ladies' favorite. Whenever he appeared, the crowd went wild.

"Men are often criticized for thinking with the little brain in their pants, but when I look at these women, I swear we're no better!" Talie admitted, eyes fixed on the stage, where the girls desperately vied for a chance to join him.

A stunning blonde holding a hundred-dollar bill between her immaculate teeth caught Jesse's attention. With a teasing grin, he approached her, easily lifting her to the stage as he claimed the money. Laying her down, he began a simulated, torrid embrace that seemed to last forever, his movements both sensual and commanding.

"We might see you in that act someday," Rebecca joked.

"Unless I start waving wads of cash in front of him, there's little chance you'll ever see me up there."

"Who knows?"

The two friends fell silent, completely captivated by Jesse's performance. Every movement was a masterclass in seduction—provocative, fluid, and utterly magnetic. Neither dared to speak or even glance at each other, afraid they might miss even the smallest beat of his mesmerizing routine. When he finally finished, he scooped the dazed blonde into his arms and carried her off the stage as the crowd erupted into thunderous applause.

"Lychee martini," the waiter said, setting the drink on their table.

Rebecca paid for her cocktail and smiled at him, leaving a generous tip. He nodded appreciatively, throwing her a flirtatious wink as he walked away.

"It's about time I take that one home," she confided, her gaze following him to the bar.

"Even with that sultry look, you'll need to step up your game," Talie laughed, sipping her drink.

"Don't challenge me!" she said, signaling for the waiter again. She brushed her hair back, letting it cascade down her voluptuous chest, and adjusted her posture confidently. As he approached their table, she licked her lips and pulled up her skirt slightly before crossing her legs. Their eyes met, hers sparkling with a playful gleam, daring him to resist.

"I'll also take five kamikaze shots," she added, her long nails brushing close to her cleavage while Talie struggled to hide her amusement.

"Perfect," he replied, his gaze lingering on her delicate

fingers before sweeping over her form. He walked away with a noticeable hunger in his expression, and Rebecca shot her friend a triumphant smile.

"Looks like you hit the mark this time," Talie said.

Rebecca grinned, a spark of confidence lighting up her face. "I've always known I'm irresistible," she laughed, licking her lips.

While Talie discreetly scanned the crowd for her favorite dancer, a warm touch brushed against her bare shoulder. Her breath hitched at the sight of Jesse standing before her, his intense eyes locking onto hers. "Come with me," he murmured, his voice low and inviting, as he extended his hand.

For a split second, a rush of excitement and anxiety surged through her. She threw a quick glance at her friend, mumbling a few incoherent words before Jesse led her away from the envious stares of the clients. They climbed a set of stairs and entered a private lounge, where the music played softly, setting a sultry tone. The dim lighting cast mysterious shadows, blurring the room's edges and making it hard for Talie to tell if they were truly alone.

The air was thick with anticipation, each note of the music weaving a spell that heightened her senses and sent her heart racing even faster. She could feel the tension between them, electric and undeniable. Jesse guided her to a plush chair and knelt before her, his hands sliding over her shoulders, brushing aside her long brown hair. His gaze lingered on her chest, where her breath rose and fell in uneven rhythms, betraying her attempt to stay composed. When his piercing blue eyes finally met hers, the heat in them burned away any pretense of distance.

"You are stunning," he murmured, the weight of his words settling deep within her.

Talie's breath hitched, her throat tightening under his unwavering stare. She had admired him countless times before, but this was different—intimate, personal. The air between them seemed to ignite, each second pulling them closer into a world where nothing else mattered. Jesse leaned in, his breath brushing against the sensitive curve of her neck, and his hand trailed lightly over her bare thigh, his touch sending shockwaves of heat through her body. A spark flared in his eyes, and in that moment, she realized she was stepping into uncharted territory, complicit in something he wasn't supposed to do: touch clients during private dances.

"Why don't you give me your number?" he whispered, his lips grazing the shell of her ear, the words a seductive caress.

Her heart clenched, her defenses momentarily faltering under the intensity of his proximity. "You don't need my number," she replied, her voice quieter than she intended. "There are plenty of girls out there waiting for you, ready to pay for a night with you."

"It's you I want," he said without hesitation, his tone steady and resolute. As he stood, the soft lighting cast shadows across his sculpted body, each line and ridge accentuated in stark relief.

She watched, enthralled, as he moved back toward the stool. With that same slow, sensual confidence she had seen so many times before, he ran his hands over his torso. But this time, every motion felt like it was meant for her. Her eyes followed the path of his fingers as they skimmed over his chest, down the defined ridges of his abs, and lingered teasingly at the waistband of his pants. A wave of heat rushed through her, and she flushed, caught off guard by the intensity of her own reaction.

She tried to look away, desperate to steady herself, but her gaze betrayed her, drawn irresistibly back to him. His eyes found hers again, locking her in place with a look so intense it felt as if he could see straight through her. The room seemed to dissolve around them, leaving only the two of them in a charged silence, suspended in a world of their own.

When the song ended, the connection between them remained unbroken, their gazes still locked in a wordless exchange.

"I am patient and very persistent," he said, his voice low, filled with the kind of promise that left her breathless.

With a subtle gesture, he extended his hand, beckoning her to follow him back to the main room, where the crowd clamored for his attention. His fingers curled around hers, warm and firm, as he led her through the sea of envious gazes. When they reached her table, he didn't release her hand right away. Instead, he leaned in and kissed her on both cheeks, his lips lingering just long enough to leave a whisper of warmth on her skin, a sensation she knew would haunt her long after he pulled away.

"Becca! You know I hate this…" she burst out the moment he was gone.

"I swear I didn't set anything up!" her friend protested, taking a long sip of her drink.

"You didn't pay him?" she asked, still confused, her brows knitting in suspicion.

"No!"

Talie's gaze shifted toward the table next to hers, where Jesse stood half-naked on a low bench, surrounded by a circle of admiring clients. His body gleamed under the club's soft lights, each movement fluid, each smile crafted to captivate. But for Talie, the sight ignited a sharp pang of misery. She hated the way these women threw themselves at him, their laughter and flirtations loud and insistent, their intentions unmistakable.

It stung even more after her intimate moment in the private lounge, where, for a fleeting time, she had allowed herself to forget the stark reality of his profession.

"I think we need to start going out to real bars," Talie muttered, fiddling with her colorful nails. "Someplace where we can meet guys who don't sell their bodies for a living."

Rebecca let out a soft laugh, arching a perfectly manicured brow. "You're saying that? You? Girl, you must have a short memory. The last time we went dancing, you were the first one hyping up the group to end the night here.”

“I was too drunk.”

“And you wouldn’t stop talking about how Jesse was under your skin and how one day, you’d have him all to yourself.”

“I was too drunk, I told you!”

Rebecca smirked knowingly, leaning closer. “I find it hard to believe you could just walk away from all of this… and him.”

“Good evening, ladies,” a familiar voice interrupted. Tristan, one of their friend’s favorite dancers, appeared beside their table with an easy smile that lit up the room.

“Good evening,” Talie replied politely, while Rebecca shot him a sly half-smile.

“Claudia isn’t here tonight?”

“No, she couldn’t make it.”

“Say hi to her for me,” he said, his eyes lingering on Rebecca before he was called over by another client.

“Claudia’s going to love that he asked about her,” Rebecca said, twirling a strand of her blonde hair absently.

But Talie barely heard her. Her attention had drifted back to Jesse, who now stood facing her with a dazzling smile, his lips curved in that sensual way that made him utterly irresistible.

He wasn’t Club Viator’s most popular dancer for nothing. Every movement of his body radiated confidence and sensuality, his sculpted muscles rippling beneath his tanned skin as if he was made to be admired.

Noticing her friend's distraction, Rebecca followed Talie's gaze and smirked knowingly. "Desire, when it gets us…" she said with a playful wink, teasing her friend about her obvious fixation on Jesse.

"Everything I know about him is so superficial."

"Well, it's hard to have a deep conversation with a guy parading half-naked in front of you," Rebecca quipped, her gaze following Jesse while he finished up and turned to greet a client.

"I know," she sighed, just when the host shouted, "Ladies, it's time to kick up those heels and dance to the best music in town!" Madonna's 'Into the Groove' blasted through the club, electrifying the atmosphere as women rushed toward the stage.

Rebecca flashed Talie a grin, adjusted her plunging neckline, and after downing another drink, they wove through the crowd, moving to the beat of the music and having the time of their lives. Their youth and beauty made them the center of attention, in stark contrast to the other regulars, whose tired faces and wrinkles told stories of years spent hoping for their favorite dancer's attention. Years spent parting with their hard-earned money for a few dances and fleeting smiles.

Talie and Rebecca knew the looks of envy directed their way, but they didn't care. They danced as if the club belonged to them, lost in their own bubble of fun, while the dancers enjoyed a break in their lounge.

Song after song fueled their euphoria until Talie, emboldened by the night's energy, caught Rebecca's eye with a mischievous grin. Without hesitation, she hiked her dress just enough to hint at her toned thighs and made her way toward the pole usually reserved for dancers. She twirled around it, her movements smooth and seductive, adding a playful but undeniably provocative flair to each spin. Rebecca laughed out loud, her eyes sparkling with delight as she watched her friend steal the attention of the crowd. The reactions from other women were mixed; some looked at her with disdain, while others cheered her on, clapping and encouraging her to continue.

As Talie performed one of her more complex spins, she glanced up and froze. Standing at the door of the dancers' lounge was Jesse, arms folded across his bare chest, his expression caught between amusement and intrigue. Their eyes locked, and a wave of heat flooded her cheeks. Her playful confidence crumbled, a flush of embarrassment creeping over her. She stepped away from the pole, smoothing her dress with trembling hands.

"You're on fire, girl!" Rebecca shouted as they returned to their table, her voice brimming with excitement.

Talie buried her face in her hands, groaning. "I thought I was going to die when I realized he was watching me."

"You've definitely got a natural talent for the pole. I bet Jesse was picturing you showing off those moves on a very different kind of pole," she teased, her laughter wicked.

"Becca!" her friend hissed, her cheeks burning brighter.

"Any lucky guy ever gotten the full show?"

Before Talie could reply, the host's voice cut through the music. "Ladies, please take your seats and give a warm welcome to Tristan!" A chorus of excited screams erupted from the crowd as Tristan took the stage.

Talie watched him for a few seconds before her interest faded. Her gaze drifted, searching for the one who troubled her more than she dared to admit.

"I'm going to the bathroom," Rebecca said, smoothing down the curve of her tight dress and adjusting her long hair. Talie nodded absently, her mind already elsewhere as she scanned the room.

At a nearby table, a group of women were laughing loudly, fidgeting with excitement while whispering among themselves. Curious, Talie tuned in to their conversation, her lips twitching into a smile upon realizing they were talking about Jesse. Their excited voices were filled with fantasies, each trying to outdo the others with the wild scenarios they dreamed of playing out with him. Their enthusiasm was infectious, and yet, as Talie listened, she felt something stir within her—a flicker of jealousy, perhaps, or a sharper, more elusive pang that left her chest tight.

Just then, her gaze instinctively sought him out, and when their eyes met again, everything else faded away. It was as if the world had narrowed to just the two of them.

"Did I miss anything?" Rebecca's voice shattered the

spell, and Talie blinked, pulled abruptly back to reality as her friend returned to the table.

"Nothing special on stage. Tristan's dancing…. lacks coordination."

Rebecca smirked knowingly. "Right now, the best show in town is happening right next to you." She nodded toward Jesse, flashing her friend a grin.

Talie followed her gaze and shifted slightly in her chair, angling herself for a better view. When she saw Jesse getting ready for another performance, her lips curved into a soft smile. "Indeed."

"You're about to have a front-row seat to his butt the entire time!"

"And I won't be the only one," she replied, noticing the other tables turning their attention toward him.

Standing confidently on his small platform, Jesse's body was a tantalizing display of controlled power. Every movement, every subtle shift of his hips or stretch of his muscles, seemed calculated to draw his audience in, leaving them spellbound. Talie's breath hitched as she watched him, unable to look away. The way his body moved—it was almost hypnotic.

"Was it like this in the private lounge earlier?" Rebecca asked, leaning in with interest.

"Not exactly…"

Rebecca raised an eyebrow, her smirk deepening. "Hotter?" she pressed, finishing the last sip of her drink.

Talie smirked. "Much hotter," she admitted, though she hated how much those private moments with Jesse lingered in her thoughts, their intensity leaving her flustered and aching for more.

As her gaze drifted back to him, she watched him slowly peel off his shirt, his muscles flexing under the dim, golden lights. He flashed her a grin, the kind of grin so tempting it could have melted even the most virtuous heart. Her lips curved into a coy smile as she took a slow, steady sip of her cocktail, trying—and failing—to distract herself from the magnetic pull of his gaze. The heat rising to her cheeks betrayed her composure, and she quickly looked down, fiddling with her glass in an attempt to ground herself. But it was futile; every fiber of her being was attuned to him, captivated by his every move.

Her resolve wavered, her eyes irresistibly drawn back to him. She caught him just as his hands moved to unbutton his pants, the slow, teasing pace sending a jolt of nervous energy coursing through her. Her pulse quickened, and as if drawn by an unseen force, her gaze darted upward to meet his—only to find him already watching her. His eyes sparkled with a knowing, teasing smirk, reading straight through the veil of confidence she wore, past the guarded facade to the vulnerable yearning she tried so hard to hide.

"If he had to choose someone tonight, I'm sure it would be you," Rebecca whispered.

Talie let out a sharp laugh, shaking her head, her voice

betraying a lack of conviction. "You're crazy. He's probably giving another girl that same look right now, making her feel just as special."

"I don't think so." Her tone was matter-of-fact, laced with an unshakable confidence.

Talie's smile faltered as Jesse's words echoed in her mind: *It's you I want*. The memory sent a flutter of something dangerously close to hope spiraling through her chest, and she hated how easily it unsettled her.

"And even if you were right, what difference would it make?"

Rebecca smirked again, her eyes glittering mischievously. "Ask your body. It hasn't had sex in two years."

Talie bit her lip, trying to suppress the pang of truth in her friend's words. The tension between her desires and her doubts felt like a storm raging inside her, pulling her in conflicting directions. She couldn't bring herself to argue, not when Jesse's pants slid lower, revealing his perfectly sculpted thighs. His gaze locked onto hers, burning with a daring intensity that left her breathless. She wanted to look away, to distance herself from the magnetic pull of his presence, but she couldn't. His movements were a symphony of temptation, every subtle shift igniting a fire that spread through her like wildfire.

"You're missing out on something big," Rebecca teased, her grin widening with the cleverness of her pun.

"You're exhausting me."

She turned her attention back to Jesse, watching as he greeted his client with that same dazzling smile that always made her chest ache. A sudden wave of fatigue washed over her, heavier than she'd expected. She was tired—tired of coming to the club week after week, chasing a fleeting thrill that always left her with a hollow emptiness in the days that followed. *A real drug*, she thought bitterly, feeling the addictive pull deep in her soul—the rush of excitement, the electricity in the air, and then the inevitable crash.

She let out a long sigh and turned to her friend. "I'm done for the night. What about you?"

Rebecca's gaze drifted to the handsome waiter lingering by the bar, his tall, muscular frame illuminated by the club's moody, soft lights. A sly smile crept across her lips. "Never enough."

"I believe you," she muttered as she observed her friend's obvious delight.

Despite her exhaustion, Talie couldn't completely dismiss the magnetic pull of the club. The low hum of desire buzzed through the air like a constant rhythm, drawing her in even when she wanted to resist. It was a world that promised so much but always left her wanting more, a world she both loved and loathed in equal measure.

"Sunny Road Agency, good morning," Talie said, her voice steady despite the sluggishness lingering from the late night. She jotted a note in her planner. "At 5 PM. Thank you," she finished, hanging up the phone and stretching in her chair, trying to shake off the tension in her shoulders.

"Did you go to Club Viator again?" Laurence, one of her colleagues, asked, leaning against the doorframe of Talie's office as she passed by.

"Yeah."

"Didn't you say last week you were done with that place?"

"I know, but when Friday night comes, and I'm pacing around my apartment like a caged lion, I always give in…"

"And your favorite?" Claudia, another colleague and self-proclaimed Viator regular, popped her head into the room, her mischievous grin impossible to miss. "He was there?"

"Oh, he was there," Talie replied, her voice dropping just slightly. "Hotter than ever." Her eyes unfocused for a moment, staring dreamily at the surface of her desk as her mind replayed flashes of last night.

Like every week, her late-night weariness and bitterness had faded by morning, leaving only the sweet taste of the seduction game imprinted on her mind.

"Hey, girls!" Rebecca said, breezing into the office, her energy as lively as ever.

"Hey, Becca! Crazy night?" Laurence asked with a knowing smirk.

"Depends on who you ask," she replied, winking in Talie's direction. "I think our dear Talie is firmly in the sights of Viator's golden boy." She used an exaggerated accent, shimmying her hips as if imitating one of the dancers.

"Things are heating up at the club!" Laurence added, her laughter chiming in like a bell.

"Little shoulder touches, knowing smiles, free private dances," Rebecca listed off, grinning wickedly.

"He does that with all the clients!" Talie protested, her cheeks betraying her as they turned a deep shade of red, vivid memories surging forward—Jesse's hands firm against her waist, the heat of his breath ghosting over her neck.

"Who are you trying to convince, girl?" Rebecca said, flipping her hair back and adjusting her tight sweater in a way that made her cleavage even more pronounced.

"I know you all went yesterday," Claudia cut in, "but I missed out. It's been two whole weeks since I last saw my Tristan," she pouted, crossing her arms in mock frustration.

Rebecca's eyes glinted with amusement. "Speaking of Tristan, he asked about you."

"He did?" Claudia's face lit up, her expression as sweet as syrup. "How adorable," she cooed, batting her lashes.

"Forget about me. Maybe next time," Laurence said, feigning work at her desk.

"Oh no, you don't!" Claudia countered, sprinting after her with determination. "You're not getting away this time!"

"Don't tell me you're all actually ready to go again tonight?" Laurence groaned, shooting them a mock glare.

Rebecca's laughter filled the room. "Our record is four nights in a row! You've got nothing to worry about." She turned to Talie, her eyes twinkling with mischief. "Are you coming tonight?"

Talie's jaw dropped, her protest caught halfway in her throat. "You're joking, right?" She couldn't believe she was getting dragged into this again, but then, flashes of memory hit her—Jesse, in the dim glow of the private lounge, his body close, his breath hot and teasing against her skin, his touch igniting a spark that still simmered beneath her surface. A shiver rippled through her despite herself.

"One day, you girls are going to pay for my addiction," she said with a sigh, giving in to the temptation once more.

Two

The doorbell chimed, breaking the stillness of Talie's apartment. She rushed to the door, her heels clicking lightly against the floor.

"Hey girl!" her friends greeted her, their voices filled with excitement as they stepped inside.

Rebecca's gaze swept over Talie's turquoise strapless top. "Someone's going to lose their mind when they see you in that outfit. I bet you'll be making a few extra trips to the private lounge tonight."

Talie laughed, pulling each of them into a quick hug. "He'll probably have a line of admirers waiting for him."

"More like a gaggle of desperate girls," Rebecca smirked.

"Becca, you're terrible!" Talie said before disappearing into the bathroom. "I'm almost done. Just give me a minute!"

Rebecca called after her. "Come on! You know Jesse only has eyes for you. The way he looks at you? He's a man on a mission."

Talie scoffed through the door, trying to brush off the comment, but a flicker of heat warmed her cheeks. "Sure, sure. Whatever you say."

In the bathroom, she leaned close to the mirror, her fingers steady as she drew a sleek black line along her eyelids. A sweep of bronze shadow followed, making her green eyes glow with a luminous vibrancy. Shaking out her long, dark hair, she adjusted the curve of her new Brazilian panties beneath her miniskirt, a small smile playing on her lips as she admired her reflection. Her multicolored heels added just the right pop of flair, elongating her legs, which already looked impossibly striking.

Rebecca popped her head in, giving Talie's butt a playful swat. "Girl, you look perfect. Let's get this party started!"

The car hummed with energy, cruising through the city. Laurence sang a nostalgic 90s song from the passenger seat, her voice off-key but bursting with enthusiasm.

"I still can't believe you're coming tonight!" Talie said as she was driving.

"Neither can I."

"And you're finally going to meet Jesse—the guy she's always raving about," Claudia added with a knowing look. "And my Tristan too!"

Rebecca leaned in from the backseat. "Let's hope, for everyone's sake, they're both there tonight."

When they arrived, the parking lot was alive with activity. A group of girls clustered near the entrance, fixing their hair and adding the final touches to their lipstick as they angled for a spot at the front of the line. Talie parked, stole one last glance in the mirror, and tucked a stray strand of hair behind her ear. A thrill of anticipation buzzed through her as she stepped out, her friends following close behind.

"Is it always this busy?" Laurence asked, her eyes darting around at the packed scene.

"It's Saturday!" Rebecca shouted back, her voice full of excitement.

Claudia practically glowed, bouncing on her toes. "This is *the* night!"

Talie couldn't help but laugh. "Looks like your two-week detox didn't last long," she teased. "You're like a kid in a candy store."

Claudia laughed and, with the carefree energy of a child, skipped ahead to join the line. As the group approached, the bouncer's eyes lit up with recognition. His weathered face softened into a warm smile as he stepped toward them. "How many tonight?" he asked, his deep voice carrying over the low thrum of the music inside.

"Four," Talie replied.

"Right this way," he said, lifting the velvet rope to let them through.

Talie flashed a grin at her friends as they entered the club. *Sometimes, being a regular has its perks*, she thought. The bouncer escorted them to a prime table, removing the "Reserved" sign before gesturing for them to sit. As he accepted a generous tip from Rebecca, he offered a nod and wished them a wonderful evening.

"Welcome to Club Viator," Claudia said to Laurence, whose eyes were wide, taking in the vibrant scene.

"You girls are VIPs now?" Laurence asked, her eyes scanning the dimly lit room as the music pulsed around them.

"Sometimes," Rebecca replied with a sly grin. "Especially when the bouncer recognizes us from the night before."

Laurence raised an eyebrow, her curiosity piqued. "So, where's this Jesse guy I've heard so much about?"

"With the description I gave you, you shouldn't have any trouble spotting him," Talie said, her gaze flicking toward the bar in anticipation.

"Tall, muscular, tan and piercing blue eyes," Laurence repeated. "Blonde hair too, right? Wait… I see one back there, but he looks old. Definitely not him."

"He's not here yet, but mine is coming!" Rebecca cheered as her favorite waiter approached.

"Good evening, ladies," he greeted them with a smile. "Can I get you something to drink?"

"A Mojito," Laurence said, her voice clipped as she tried to focus on the cocktail menu rather than his biceps.

"Cosmopolitan for me," Claudia replied.

"You," Rebecca whispered in Talie's ear, barely holding back her laughter.

"Lychee martini for you, ladies?" he asked, glancing at the duo.

"Yes," they answered in unison, giggling like schoolgirls caught in a moment of guilty pleasure. His smile deepened, adding just the right amount of charm, before he said, "I'll be right back."

Laurence arched an eyebrow. "Wow, a club where the waiter knows your drink? That says a lot about how often you girls come here."

"Trust me, we're well aware," Talie replied with a playful eye roll.

Before Laurence could press further, the music cut off, replaced by the sultry voice of the evening's host. "Ladies, we've got a special show for you tonight!" The lights dimmed, smoke swirled, and five dancers dressed as firefighters stormed the stage, their entrance igniting the room with energy.

Talie's heart pounded, her gaze sweeping over the performers, hoping to catch a glimpse of Jesse amid the electrifying chaos.

Claudia nudged Laurence. "See the guy on the right?"

"The one with the tattoo?"

"Yeah, that's Tristan," she said, her voice brimming with pride.

Laurence gave him a once-over, her lips curving into a smirk. "Not my type… way too bulky."

Claudia gasped in mock offense. "Too bulky?!"

"He looks like he's been living in the gym… or on steroids. Just too big for me."

"As long as 'too big' isn't packed in his underwear!" Rebecca quipped, sending the group into peals of laughter.

As the sexy firefighters riled up the crowd with provocative moves, Laurence's attention wandered toward the bar. Her breath hitched when she spotted him—a tall, magnetic figure with sun-kissed blonde hair and a golden snake bracelet coiled around his powerful forearm. His physique was stunning, his pants hanging low on his hips, perfectly showcasing the deep V of his abs that disappeared beneath the waistband. As if sensing her gaze, he turned, locking eyes with her for a split second. The intensity in that one glance ignited a thrill that coursed through her, leaving her pulse racing.

"Talie, is Jesse wearing a snake bracelet by any chance?"

"Yes," Talie replied, her own breath catching as her gaze followed Laurence's. And there he was, standing by the bar, his presence impossible to ignore.

The waiter returned just then, setting their drinks on the table. Rebecca paid for the drinks and slid him a generous tip, her fingers grazing his forearm just long enough to leave an impression.

"It's a pleasure," he said smoothly, his eyes flashing with playful intent before he walked away.

Rebecca smiled, raising her glass, "I'm so excited we're all here tonight. Let's drink to that!"

"Cheers," they echoed, clinking their glasses together.

Talie took a slow sip of her lychee martini, the sweet, floral taste mingling with the warmth spreading through her from the alcohol. Just as she lowered her glass, a familiar, warm hand slid over her shoulder. Each time, she knew it was him, his very personal way of welcoming her.

Turning her head, she met his magnetic gaze. His lips curved into that signature smirk, the one that made her pulse race. Leaning closer, he brought his lips near her ear, his breath warm against her skin. "Are you going to dazzle us with another performance tonight?"

Caught off guard, Talie felt a blush creeping up her cheeks. "I don't think so," she replied softly, her voice barely audible over the pounding music.

"Shame," he said, his eyes sweeping over her with an intensity that made her knees weak. "You were very sexy."

The way he looked at her, as if peeling back her layers, left her breathless. Her friends watched the exchange intently, their interest written all over their faces.

"Later," he added before flashing a grin at her friends and walking away, his broad shoulders cutting through the crowd.

Talie let out a shaky sigh, her heart pounding as she watched him retreat to the bar. It took a moment to steady herself, but her reprieve was short-lived. Laurence leaned in, her grin wide and teasing. "Your Jesse's gorgeous! What did he whisper in your ear?"

"Nothing important," she said, trying to play it cool, though her flushed cheeks told another story.

"Oh, come on! You can't say it was nothing," Claudia replied, her eyes sparkling with amusement.

"It's always the same," Rebecca said, taking a sip of her drink. "He comes over, whispers sweet nothings, takes her to the private lounge, but we never know what they say to each other."

Before Talie could answer, the host's voice cut through the chatter. "Ladies, give it up for the one and only Jesse!"

All four friends immediately turned toward the stage, their eyes glued to Jesse as he stepped into the spotlight. His movements were slow, dripping with sensuality. With each step, he commanded attention, his hands skimming over his chiseled torso, fingers brushing over taut muscles that flexed beneath the dim lights. He tousled his hair with a casual ease, the slight motion sending a ripple of excitement through the crowd.

"Wow," Laurence whispered, her eyes wide as they followed his every move.

The tempo of the music quickened, and Jesse spun around the pole with effortless strength, showing off the impressive musculature of his arms and abs. As the lights flashed, his piercing blue eyes found Talie in the crowd, locking onto her for what felt like an eternity. She didn't flinch, but her three friends couldn't hide their reactions.

"He's definitely looking at you!" Laurence said, her voice a mix of surprise and envy.

"Don't be ridiculous!" Talie laughed, her heart racing with excitement.

"Ridiculous?" Claudia echoed, shaking her head. "Talie, half the women in here would sell their souls for the way he just looked at you. Own it!"

Talie looked at her friend and smiled. A sincere smile that spoke volumes about her confused, even repressed, emotions. She didn't want to admit how different Jesse treated her. The idea of acknowledging it scared her—the passion, the intensity, it was almost too much to bear.

"Everything okay, ladies?" the waiter asked as he cleared some glasses from their table. His gaze lingered on Rebecca, who had been unabashedly flirting with him all evening.

"We're ready for another round," Rebecca said, her tone dripping with suggestion as she handed him another generous tip. Her fingers brushed his, a bold move that earned her a sly smirk in return.

The night unfolded like a decadent dream. Drinks flowed freely, laughter echoed above the thrum of music, and the seductive energy of the club buzzed in the air like static electricity. Shows came and went, blending into the intoxicating atmosphere, but the four friends were lost in their own world—swapping stories and secrets.

Claudia was about to order another round when Talie waved her off. "I'm driving, girls! You can keep going, but I'm officially out," she said, shaking her head with a laugh.

"Waiter! Three shooters! Your choice!" Claudia called, her voice already thick with alcohol.

"Make it four," Rebecca giggled, leaning back in her seat.

The waiter chuckled, clearly entertained, and disappeared toward the bar, but not before throwing Rebecca a lingering glance that made her preen with delight. "Did you see that? He's totally into me," she declared, leaning forward as if to include them in her conspiratorial triumph.

Laurence laughed, her eyes tracing one of the dancers performing a slow, provocative routine nearby. "Isn't it amazing to ogle these gorgeous men without guilt? Best free show in town."

"It's even better when you're close enough to touch," Rebecca added, waggling her eyebrows. "If you had to pick one, who would it be?"

Laurence didn't miss a beat. "I know Jesse's your favorite, Talie, but let's be real. He's the hottest guy here."

Talie gave her a knowing glance, then turned to Rebecca. "She's going to kill you," she whispered.

A few minutes later, Claudia and Laurence excused themselves to freshen up, leaving Talie and Rebecca alone. As soon as they were out of earshot, Rebecca leaned in.

"Okay, listen," she whispered. "It's Laurence's first time here, and I really want her to get *the* full experience."

Talie arched an eyebrow. "I know that look, and I know exactly what you're planning."

Rebecca's grin widened, unrepentant. "So, you're okay with it?"

Talie hesitated, the image of Jesse's teasing smile flashing through her mind. "I'm not thrilled about the idea of him dancing for someone else at my table," she admitted, her voice softer now. "But if it's for Laurence, fine. At least I'll still get to enjoy the show."

Rebecca flashed her a wicked grin and slipped away before she could change her mind, weaving through the crowd until she caught Jesse on his way backstage. By the time Claudia and Laurence returned, glowing and giggling from their trip to the bathroom, Rebecca had already set her plan in motion.

"Well, girls, I have to admit," Laurence began as she slid back into her seat, "you were right. I've been seriously missing out by not coming here these past few months."

"We told you!" they all shouted.

"Trust me," Rebecca said, her grin taking on an edge of sly anticipation, "you haven't seen anything yet."

Just as she finished speaking, Jesse appeared, his confident stride drawing all attention to their table. His piercing blue eyes swept over the group before he leaned in, greeting Laurence with a charming smile and a kiss on each cheek. The warmth of his touch lingered, and her stunned expression sent the rest of the group into fits of giggles.

"Jesse," he introduced himself smoothly, his voice low and captivating, as if his presence alone could command the room.

Laurence, still recovering from the surprise, stammered a greeting while shooting her friends a betrayed look. The girls, unable to contain their laughter, teased her with playful nudges, thoroughly enjoying the moment.

But while the others basked in the spectacle, Talie's attention was drawn to Jesse in a different way. As he climbed onto his bench, her eyes followed the line of his neck down the broad expanse of his back, lingering on the firm curve of his butt and the strong, defined muscles of his thighs. Every movement he made was deliberate, as if he knew exactly how much power each subtle motion held. She was captivated, drawn back into his orbit, all over again. And then, his gaze found hers.

It was as if the world had stopped spinning. The laughter of her friends, the cheers from the crowd—all of it dissolved into the background. Her breath hitched, her pulse quickened. His eyes lingered on hers, electric and consuming, holding her in place with an intensity that left her no choice but to surrender. She felt exposed as if he could see through every layer she'd carefully built around herself. For those few moments, she was his, completely and undeniably.

As the music slowed and his routine ended, Jesse leaned down to kiss Laurence's cheeks once more, eliciting a delighted squeal from her. His grin was playful, but just before he walked away, he shot Talie one last look, his eyes lingering in a way that set her heart racing. She watched him disappear into the crowd, the moment slipping through her fingers like a dream she wasn't ready to wake up from.

"Oh my God!" Laurence finally gasped, breaking the silence at the table. "I can't believe you set me up!" she said, still trying to process what had just happened.

"Welcome to Club Viator experience," Rebecca quipped, raising her glass. "You only get one first time, and we made sure it was unforgettable," she added as the host's voice echoed through the speakers, pulling her attention. "Ladies, it's time to book your favorite dancers for the final part of the evening," he announced, sending a wave of excitement through the crowd.

Still shaken, Laurence turned back to her friends. "I understand why you're so obsessed with Jesse, but honestly, some women spend their entire paycheck here just to feel noticed by these guys. I mean, it's sad when you think about it."

Talie nodded absently, her gaze still locked on Jesse. "It's more than being noticed," she murmured, almost to herself.

"Have you ever slow-danced with him?" Laurence asked, a hint of curiosity in her tone.

Talie hesitated, her fingers lightly tracing the rim of her glass. "Becca paid for it once during our first visits here, but not since. We usually leave before it gets to that point. Tonight's different because you're here."

As if on cue, the music swelled, a sultry rhythm filling the air, and couples began to take the stage under the eager gaze of the audience. Jesse was among them, his presence magnetic even on a crowded stage. He danced with a young woman whose plunging neckline left little to the imagination. Her movements were bold, her hands trailing over his chiseled torso as she leaned into him, her intentions unmistakable. She angled herself, drawing his attention to her assets, clearly vying for his favor.

The four friends watched the spectacle, their commentary flowing freely as they took in the sight of women indulging in the evening's luxury. "I guess it's the only way to get close to them," Laurence noted, eyeing the girl who ran her hands over the defined muscles of Jesse's back. "Can you even do that in the private lounge?"

"No," Talie replied, her eyes lingering on the girl's hand as it drifted to the nape of Jesse's neck. The image stirred something in her—a flicker of envy she didn't want to acknowledge.

Her mind drifted back to a memory of their bodies moving in perfect rhythm during their only slow dance. She could still feel his warm breath on her skin, the way their connection was wordless, communicated solely through their shared gaze. She remembered the softness of his lips brushing against her cheeks as he leaned in to ask for her name.

"Talie."

"I'm Jesse," he had said, his sparkling blue eyes locking onto hers with a promise she couldn't quite decipher. "Hope to see you again."

The memory washed over her, the echo of that moment still strong enough to make her pulse race.

"Shall we go, girls?" Claudia asked, pulling her back to the present.

"Agreed," Laurence mumbled, stifling a yawn as she reached for her bag.

As they began gathering their things, the song came to an end, and Jesse escorted the young woman back to her seat. Talie couldn't help but track his every movement, her breath hitching slightly when he turned in their direction. Instead of disappearing backstage, he headed toward their table, his stride confident.

"He's coming over!" Rebecca whispered, her excitement barely contained.

Talie felt a sudden rush of nerves as she looked up, catching sight of him approaching. Their eyes locked, and in that moment, she felt it again—the magnetic pull that made her feel like resistance was futile. Her breath caught, and when he stopped beside her, extending his hand, her hesitation lasted only a heartbeat before she slipped her fingers into his.

As he led her toward the stage, she felt his gaze sweep over her, lingering on every curve with a quiet intensity. Ascending the steps, she caught the slight nod he gave her, his eyes gleaming with approval. Her cheeks flushed under his scrutiny, but the flutter of excitement in her chest only grew.

"It's unusual to see you here this late," he said, his voice low and smooth, curling around her like smoke.

"Yeah, I know."

"I'm glad you're here. You spice up my nights," he said, taking her waist with his large hands and pulling her closer.

Her arms hesitantly looped around his neck, her breath hitching while she avoided his piercing gaze. The tension was palpable, humming in the space between them as their movements melded into a shared rhythm.

"I wish I could see you more often," he whispered in her ear, his breath warm and enticing.

"More often?" she laughed softly. "Jesse, I'm here every week."

"Who else do you leave behind when you come here?" he asked, his eyes studying her.

"No one."

"Then why not?" he pressed, his tone calm but insistent. "Just meet me somewhere else."

She glanced down, her eyes landing on the defined muscles of his chest. "Forget it," she murmured.

"Talie," he said, her name a low rumble that seemed to vibrate through her, "when I say you spice up my nights, I mean it. I want to know more about you."

His hands slid lower, tracing the curve of her back and pausing just above her hips. The gentle pressure sent a rush of heat through her, and before she could stop herself, her body leaned into his, her face brushing against the warmth of his neck. His scent—an intoxicating mix of cologne and something distinctly him—wrapped around her like a spell. Her lips grazed his skin, moving in sync with the slow rhythm of his body swaying against hers.

"Your lips," he murmured, his voice a deep, seductive hum that stirred something primal within her. "They're giving me all kinds of ideas."

Her breath caught as his words sank in, and she instinctively pulled back, her eyes darting to his neck, where the faintest trace of her lipstick marked his skin, a tangible reminder of their closeness.

Jesse's lips curled into a teasing smile. "I don't know what you've got planned after the club closes," he said, his tone light yet laced with desire, "but I'd love to take you back to my place and show you what I'm thinking."

Talie's heart pounded, her thoughts a tangled mess as she struggled to find her voice. His eyes held hers, a quiet challenge flickering in their depths, daring her to break through her own walls.

"I…" she began, her voice barely a whisper. She averted her eyes, overwhelmed by the intensity of his gaze, feeling herself unravel under it. "I can't," she finally said.

"Are you sure?" he asked, a smile tugging at the corners of his lips.

Seconds stretched into what felt like an eternity before she finally summoned the courage to speak. "Yes, I'm sure."

"It feels like your body's saying something entirely different."

He was right. He knew exactly how she felt, but she couldn't bring herself to admit it—not to him, and certainly not to herself. How could she be so caught up in someone she barely knew? An exotic dancer, no less.

The words hung in the air between them, yet the silence that followed only seemed to amplify the electricity sparking between their bodies. Jesse didn't pull away. Instead, he kept the rhythm of their slow, sensual dance, fully aware of the internal battle raging inside her, the one he knew far from over.

When the song finally ended, he released her with a lingering touch. Taking her hand in his, he led her back to the table, his fingers intertwining with hers in a gesture that felt far too intimate. As they reached her seat, he leaned in, brushing his lips softly against her cheek.

"Sweet dreams."

"What a night!" Claudia exclaimed as she slipped into the car, her energy crackling like static in the confined space.

"I know," Talie muttered, already bracing herself for what was coming next.

"You and Jesse!"

"Don't even go there," she replied, rubbing her temples as if the memory itself was a headache.

Claudia shot her a sideways glance. "Oh, come on. Just invite him out. You two could finally… you know, work out all that tension."

Talie let out a humorless laugh, shaking her head. "Yeah, right. Like that's going to happen."

"I'm serious! He'd say yes in a heartbeat," Claudia insisted, her excitement too much for Talie's already jumbled thoughts.

"I can't." Her voice came out sharper than she intended.

Claudia threw her hands up in exasperation. "Talie, you're out of your mind! The spark between you two could burn down this entire city, and you're just pretending it doesn't exist?"

"You girls don't get it," Rebecca interjected from the backseat. "Talie doesn't want to be just another woman in his life. She's holding back because she knows she won't get his exclusivity."

Claudia blinked, momentarily thrown off balance. "Wait… do exclusive relationships even exist anymore?"

A sharp pain twisted in Talie's chest, but she kept her eyes fixed on the road, refusing to let them see the turmoil that was tearing her apart inside.

Silence hung heavy in the air before she finally spoke, her voice quieter now. "Do you want the truth? Before Jesse, I was solid. Unshakable. No guy ever got to me the way he has—and I barely know him. I never believed in one-night stand, but now I can't stop imagining all these scenarios, all these… things. I'm questioning everything I thought I stood for. And it scares the hell out of me."

The car fell silent, her confession rippling through the air like an unspoken truth finally given voice.

"The answer is obvious, at least to me," Rebecca said gently, her tone full of certainty.

Claudia nodded. "Same here."

Even Laurence, who had stayed silent until now, spoke up. "I don't know… if I were in your shoes, I think I'd give in, too."

Talie swallowed hard, her grip tightening on the steering wheel as the weight of their words sank in. "God, help me," she whispered, so quietly it was almost lost in the hum of the engine. But the despair, the yearning—it was all there.

Three

"Did you enjoy your day off?" Rebecca asked, her eyes gleaming with curiosity as she leaned closer to Talie.

"I read a book, worked out, and tried to catch up on sleep… but my mind wouldn't let me rest," she replied with a half-smile. "What about you?"

"I worked out, ran some errands, and—you won't believe this—I bumped into David."

"David?" Talie raised an eyebrow, the name pulling her full attention.

"Yes! At the grocery store, of all places. We ended up chatting, and before I knew it, he invited me over for dinner." Rebecca's voice dripped with satisfaction, clearly relishing every detail.

"And how long has it been since you two last saw each other?"

"Four, maybe five months?"

Talie couldn't hide her smirk. "Does he know about your little fling with his friend?"

Rebecca burst into laughter. "He didn't bring it up… and I wasn't about to."

"You're something else," she said, shaking her head in disbelief.

"Do you remember David's friend was interested in you, but I was the one who ended up in his bed?" Rebecca's grin turned wicked. "And for the record, he was insanely hot. Fucked like a god."

Talie rolled her eyes but couldn't suppress a chuckle. "I told you before—I'm solid as a rock."

"Sure, sure," Rebecca teased. "But we both know everyone's got their weaknesses."

Talie cleared her throat, desperate for a subject change. "And how did your evening end?"

Rebecca leaned back, a smug look on her face. "He wants to see me again this week."

"And?"

"I told him I had a busy schedule," Rebecca said with a casual shrug.

"That sounds… cold. Like, 'You're not worth making time for.'"

Rebecca laughed, tossing her hair back. "Oh, please. Why sugarcoat it? If he can't handle honesty, that's on him."

"Becca, don't you ever think about settling down? Having something real?"

"Stability? It sounds dangerously close to boredom. Maybe I'm just wired differently. Or… maybe I need therapy?" she joked, a big smile on her face.

"Sure, I'm the crazy one here. Keep sleeping with all the men if it makes you feel better."

"Trust me. I intend to!"

Back at her desk, Talie was engrossed in work, sorting through files when the agency door creaked open. She glanced up, ready to greet the new client, but her words caught in her throat.

Standing in the doorway, with that familiar charming smile, was the waiter from Club Viator.

"Hello," she managed, her cheeks flushing as her heart skipped a beat.

"I was hoping to get some travel advice," he said, his voice smooth and warm.

Talie straightened, her professional demeanor slipping into place despite the flutter of nerves in her chest. "You've come to the right place. Follow me," she said, motioning him toward her desk.

As he settled into the chair across from her, he leaned back with an easy smile. "Been working here long?"

"A couple of years," she answered, quickly redirecting the conversation. "Where are you thinking of going?"

"The Caribbean."

"Any specific destination in mind?"

"I want something unique. Five-star accommodations, great food, and plenty of activities," he said, his tone shifting into something more focused.

"Have you considered Turks and Caicos?" she asked, her fingers already tapping at the keyboard.

"I've heard good things."

She leaned in slightly, showing him a few options on the screen. "These are some of the top luxury resorts," she explained. "Do you have a budget in mind?"

His answer was immediate. "No budget. I want the best."

Talie blinked, momentarily caught off guard by his decisiveness. As she scrolled through the options, she realized just how much he probably earned in tips, given how easily he was ready to splurge.

"And how many guests?" she asked, glancing up at him.

"Two."

Before she could respond, the glass door swung open, and Rebecca peeked in, her expression a mix of excitement and urgency. "Mr. Hudson is on the phone. He absolutely needs to know if you've got his tickets booked," she said, already halfway into the room.

"Yes, it's confirmed," Talie replied smoothly, barely suppressing a laugh at Rebecca's wide-eyed reaction to the man seated across from her. "Tell him I'll call him in an hour with all the details."

"Perfect," she said, her gaze lingering on the waiter. She gave him a quick once-over before flashing a polite smile. "Hi," she added, tucking a strand of hair behind her ear as she backed out of the office, closing the door behind her.

Talie shook her head, stifling a chuckle. "Sorry about that."

"No problem at all," he replied, his eyes glinting with amusement. "So, you're more than just regulars at Club Viator?"

Her cheeks flushed under his teasing tone. "Well, now you know."

Trying to shake off her nerves, she swiveled her computer screen toward him. "Here are two of my top resort picks," she began, pointing to the screen. "This one offers a wider range of activities, but both are incredible."

He leaned back in his chair, his eyes briefly scanning the screen before returning to hers. "Perfect."

Talie arched a brow. "You don't want to see more photos? Read some reviews? Maybe get more details?"

"Nope," he replied, his confidence unwavering. "I trust you."

Her fingers hesitated over the keyboard, her heart giving an unexpected flutter. "You're putting a lot of pressure on me," she said, trying to mask her unease. "And when are you thinking of going?"

"We'd like to leave at the end of November. A one-week trip."

She nodded, scanning for availability. "There's a direct flight on November 28th, leaving Thursday. It's a perfect match." She turned to him with a smile.

"Can you book it now?" he asked, his eagerness palpable.

"I'll need the names of both passengers and their birthdates as they appear on their passports."

"Not a problem," he said, pulling out his phone to check his notes.

Talie opened the booking form, her fingers poised over the keyboard. "I don't usually make bookings this quickly. Most clients take forever to decide," she remarked, casting him a sideways glance.

"Time is money," he replied with a playful wink.

She chuckled softly, her mind briefly drifting to how much he must earn in tips with charm like that. "All right," she said, focusing on the form. "What's the first passenger's name and birth date?"

"Me—Clayton Harlow." He spelled it out, giving her his birth date. She quickly calculated his age, realizing he was only four years older than her.

"And the second passenger?"

"Jesse Levine."

Her breath hitched, her pulse quickening. She forced herself to keep her expression neutral, though her hands trembled slightly as she typed. "Will you be making a deposit or paying in full?" she asked, her voice steadier than she expected.

"Paying in full," he replied, sliding a sleek black credit card across the desk. His gaze lingered on hers for a moment, the corner of his mouth lifting into a subtle, teasing smile.

Talie finished the transaction swiftly, her fingers dancing over the keyboard before printing out the hotel summary and receipt. "All set. I'll email you the electronic tickets as soon as they're available," she said, handing him the documents with a professional smile.

"Thank you, Talie. You're really efficient," he said, standing up and offering his hand.

"My pleasure," she replied, shaking it. But as he turned to leave, she found herself blurting out, "One more thing…did you know I worked here?"

He paused, a slow, knowing smile spreading across his face. "Let's just call it a coincidence," he said smoothly, leaving her standing there, her thoughts spinning before he disappeared through the door.

Moments later, Rebecca burst into the office like a whirlwind, her eyes wide with excitement. "Talie! Why didn't you call me the second you saw him? I could've made up some excuse to handle his booking!"

Talie laughed, still shaken from the encounter. "I know! I was so shocked I didn't even think of it."

"My jaw hit the floor when I saw him in here!" she said, collapsing into the chair across from Talie.

"It was picture-worthy,"

"What was he even doing here?" she asked, leaning forward, her curiosity insatiable.

"Booking a trip. What do you think?"

Rebecca's expression shifted to one of suspicion. "Wait… did he know we work here?"

Talie hesitated, replaying their interaction in her mind. "No idea. I asked, and he said it was a coincidence… but the way he looked at me, I don't know. It felt like he knew more than he was letting on."

Rebecca's eyes sparkled mischievously. "You think he came here on purpose?"

Talie shrugged, feigning indifference. "Who knows? But guess who he's going on vacation with."

"No way!" Rebecca's voice rose an octave, her excitement palpable.

Talie picked up the booking receipt and waved it in front of her friend. "Jesse Levine, 35 years old."

Rebecca's jaw dropped, and then she burst into laughter. "I can't believe his stage name is his real name! That's… iconic."

"It suits him perfectly!"

"You're not exactly impartial when it comes to him." Her voice carried the kind of teasing familiarity that only close friends could pull off. "And Clayton Harlow, 34… That man is pure temptation. If I'd been the one handling this booking, I'd have made it my mission to charm him. I mean, how can you call this a coincidence?"

"Stop overanalyzing it," she replied, her voice soft, almost too soft. It sounded more like she was convincing herself than her friend.

Late summer was always a slow period at the agency. Clients trickled in sporadically, flipping through brochures and daydreaming about future vacations, but hardly anyone committed to booking. Talie found the lull particularly grating, unlike her friends, who could chatter endlessly to fill the silence. This year, though, felt especially heavy—a stretch of unbroken monotony with few projects to anchor her focus.

"I hope people won't take forever to start booking their winter vacations," she muttered, glancing at her friends, who were engrossed in a glossy cruise brochure.

"Be patient," Laurence said with an easy smile, ever the optimist.

"Are you guiding any groups this fall?" Talie asked, steering the conversation toward work, hoping it might spark some inspiration.

"Nothing planned at the moment. You?" Claudia looked up, her eyes curious.

"Just a one-week tour in Mexico, but that's it," she replied, her voice tinged with frustration.

"Maybe we should take a little trip to Turks and Caicos at the end of November. What do you think, girls?" Rebecca's eyes sparkled with excitement as she made the suggestion.

"Wait, what?" Talie blinked, staring at her in disbelief.

"We've had such a rough summer! A warm getaway sounds perfect," she added, her grin widening like a conspirator revealing a master plan.

"I'd love to know what's really on your mind, Becca," Talie said, narrowing her eyes with mock suspicion.

"Oh, you already know… and you understand it perfectly."

"I think Becca's planning a little rendezvous with your handsome Jesse," Claudia teased, her raised brow adding to the mischief.

"Don't even think about it. There's no way I'm going on vacation to the Turks and Caicos at the end of November," Talie shot back, crossing her arms for emphasis.

"Vacations are perfect for getting closer. I'd definitely take advantage of that with Clayton."

"Of course you would. It'd be so subtle for us to end up at the same hotel, during the same week. Genius plan, really," she said sarcastically, rolling her eyes.

"Craziness keeps us alive. The spontaneous, the unexpected, the wild passions."

"Maybe it keeps you alive, but your head's always in the clouds," Talie retorted.

"You're right. Maybe I'm on an eternal high, but tell me, which anchor is healthier: ground or sky? I'm convinced I enjoy life more than you do, and I'm loving every minute of it," Rebecca said, twirling a lock of hair with a dreamy smile.

"Whew! This conversation's getting intense," Claudia interjected with a laugh, trying to lighten the mood.

"Real friends can say anything to each other," Talie said, feeling the warmth of their friendship.

"Confronting ideas helps you grow," Rebecca added. "So… shall we book this trip?"

Later that evening, Talie left the office, lacing up her running shoes like she did every night. Running had always been her escape, her way of clearing her head. But lately, the steady rhythm of her feet hitting the pavement couldn't drown out the storm of thoughts swirling in her mind. No matter how fast she ran, they followed her— thoughts about her life, her accomplishments, her unspoken desires… and Jesse. Everything kept circling back to him—no matter how much she tried to push him away.

"Do you realize my life revolves around our nights at the club these days?" Talie confessed, her eyes fixed on the dancers performing on stage. "Every Friday feels like a brief escape from my personal hell."

"That bad?" Rebecca's voice softened, concern threading through her words.

"I've never felt so drained, so exhausted. Club Viator gives me a boost for a few hours, but afterward, the crash is brutal."

"Damn. I had no idea you were feeling this low."

"It's worse when things are slow at work," she explained, a lump forming in her throat.

"You weren't this down last year, and God knows it was just as quiet at the end of the summer!"

"I guess there's just more on my mind this time," she whispered, her voice barely audible.

Rebecca leaned closer. "What's bothering you?"

"A lot of things," she began, but her attention shifted as she noticed their waiter approaching.

"Good evening, ladies," Clayton greeted them with a charming smile. "How are you tonight?"

"Great," they replied, exchanging a knowing look that said more than words could convey.

"The usual drinks?"

"Tonight, I'll have a Mojito," Rebecca said, her gaze lingering on his lips.

Talie lifted her chin slightly, as if that could shake off the weight pressing on her chest. "Thai Sapphire for me."

"Breaking the routine?" he teased, his glance flicking to Rebecca's short skirt.

"Sometimes, it's necessary," she quipped, her tone flirtatious.

As he walked off to the bar, Talie stifled a laugh. "I'm lucky to have you, Becca. You always know how to get my mind off things," she said, grateful for the distraction.

"You need more excitement in your life!

"I know. My life's boring."

"Well, there's a dose of excitement right ahead," she said, nudging her subtly.

Talie's gaze followed Rebecca's line of sight to where Jesse crouched next to a client, his trademark dazzling smile lighting up the room. Every inch of him exuded sensuality, but beyond that, he radiated something Talie deeply craved—genuine happiness.

"I think I'm losing my mind," she murmured, her voice barely above a whisper.

Rebecca tilted her head, her brow furrowed. "What do you mean?"

"Since we've been coming here, I've become… obsessed with Jesse," she confessed, not daring to look at her friend. "And it's getting more complicated every time."

"What do you mean obsessed?"

"Jesse wants to see me outside the club."

Rebecca's face lit up instantly. "What!"

"Becca, everything's so simple for you when sex is involved. You don't weigh the pros and cons. I'm not sure you're the best person to advise me on this…"

"Go for it!" she exclaimed, grabbing her friend's hand.

"That's exactly what I didn't want to hear!"

"It's exactly what you need to hear!" she insisted, her grip tightening as if to shake sense into her friend.

"I've spent days convincing myself that I don't really know him, that he probably tells the same stories to every girl, that I'm emotionally vulnerable, and that it's insane to get involved with an exotic dancer. But every time I see him, my heart races. I don't want just a one-night stand. I want more. I'm certain of it."

Rebecca's expression softened. "The only way to find out if there could be more is to meet him outside of the club."

"And end up with a broken heart," Talie muttered, her gaze following Jesse as he made his way to the bar.

Her confession hung heavy in the air, her words echoing in her mind. Jesse's voice, too, played on a loop. *I am patient and very persistent.* She knew his patience and persistence would eventually wear down her defenses. The only way to protect herself was to stop going to the club altogether and forget about him.

Rebecca offered her a gentle smile, her voice unusually soft. "Girl, memories are the most valuable things we hold in our hearts and minds. If you miss out on the good things in life because you're afraid of getting hurt, your heart might stay safe, but it'll be empty too."

Talie's green eyes filled with emotion, her friend's words striking a chord she hadn't expected. She opened her mouth to respond but found herself momentarily at a loss.

Rebecca chuckled lightly, breaking the tension. "I know, coming from me, it sounds crazy," she said with a self-deprecating grin, her attention shifting to the waiter as he passed by. For once, she didn't bother initiating conversation, a rare display of restraint.

They paid for their drinks, the chatter continuing to swirl around them. Yet Talie's attention drifted elsewhere, her thoughts slipping deeper into the tangle of emotions she'd been carrying. Just as she began to lose herself, a warm hand rested on her shoulder, the touch halting her mid-breath. She turned slowly, her heart skipping a beat, and found herself face-to-face with Jesse. The magnetic pull between them surged instantly, as powerful as ever.

"Good evening," he said, leaning in to kiss her cheeks, the closeness making her pulse quicken.

"Good evening," she replied softly, her voice nearly catching on the words.

"I heard Clayton managed to find you among all the agencies in town."

"It must be luck," she said, keeping her tone light. Yet there was an unspoken weight behind her words, as if the supposed coincidence carried more significance than either of them wanted to admit.

"You picked an amazing destination for us."

"I hope you'll love it," she said, her lips curving into a shy smile. But her composure faltered slightly when his gaze swept down to her miniskirt before rising to meet her eyes again.

Leaning closer, he dropped his voice to a whisper, the intimacy sending a shiver down her spine. "There's something else I'd love even more."

Talie's cheeks burned as a flush crept across her skin. She shifted subtly in her chair, tugging at the hem of her skirt in a futile attempt to compose herself. Jesse straightened, offering her one last lingering look. "See you later," he murmured, brushing a casual greeting to her friend before walking away.

Rebecca watched him retreat, then turned to Talie with an amused smirk. "Your eyes are sparkling," she teased, nudging her playfully.

"All it takes is a few words, and I forget everything."

"That's passion!"

Talie sighed, resting her chin in her palm. "Feels like a rollercoaster to me…"

As the evening wore on, she found herself craving Jesse's attention, her gaze drifting toward the stage whenever she thought she might catch a glimpse of him.

But he was in high demand—solo performances, birthday parties, and private shows. *Another busy Friday*, she thought, her heart sinking. Usually, she was lucky enough to steal at least two conversations with him in a night, but tonight, it seemed unlikely.

"It might be better if I stop coming here. I know I say this every week but today feels different."

Rebecca raised a skeptical brow. "Really?"

Talie sighed, her fingers brushing across her forehead as if she could rub away the weight of her thoughts. "I swear. I need to make a radical choice… for my mental health."

"And you think sitting at home, stuck in your apartment, won't push you into an even worse depression?"

"I don't know what to think anymore," she admitted, her voice faltering as she rubbed her face in frustration. She inhaled deeply, but the breath did little to steady the storm brewing within her. "Maybe I need therapy," she muttered, more to herself than to Rebecca.

Her heart was tangled in knots, emotions pulling her in opposite directions. She felt exhausted, caught in a tug-of-war between her heart and her head. Part of her wanted to protect herself, to shut everything out, while the other part yearned for something more—for him. And as if her silent turmoil had summoned him, Jesse appeared, his hand extended toward her. She hesitated, startled, but the warmth in his eyes left her no room to resist. Without a word, she placed her hand in his and allowed him to lead her to the private lounge.

"Jesse… I don't feel very well tonight," she confessed as they settled into the quiet room. The plush chair seemed to swallow her up, but it couldn't shield her from the vulnerability that wrapped itself around her. She could feel her emotional walls crumbling, leaving her exposed in a way that terrified her.

Jesse crouched in front of her, his piercing blue eyes scanning her face as if searching for the source of her unease. Silence enveloped them, heavy and intimate, before he finally spoke, his voice a soothing caress. "You don't have to worry. I'll take care of you," he said, the sincerity in his tone comforting. "I'll make you feel good."

Her chest tightened at his words, and she looked away. "That's what scares me," she whispered, the confession slipping out before she could stop it.

Jesse didn't move, didn't waver. "What are you really afraid of, Talie?"

Her heart raced, her thoughts spiraling. "You," she admitted, the single word trembling in the space between them.

A flicker of understanding crossed his face, but his intensity didn't diminish. "I think you're more afraid of yourself than of me," he murmured, his hands gently tracing the length of her arms before resting on her shoulders. His touch was steady, grounding. He leaned in, his breath warm against her ear, and whispered, "Let yourself go."

His lips brushed against the side of her neck, soft and unhurried, sending a wave of warmth cascading through her body. Each touch was a quiet plea, coaxing her to surrender to the moment. "I forget everything when I'm with you," she admitted, her voice barely above a breath.

Jesse's lips curved into a subtle smile against her skin as he trailed kisses along her collarbone. His hands skimmed down her thighs, fingertips barely grazing her skin before reaching her knees. With deliberate ease, he parted them, and her breath faltered. The lace of her skirt slid higher, exposing more of her bare flesh to his hungry gaze. His eyes darkened, lingering there, drinking her in, making her feel like the most intoxicating thing in the room.

"Jesse," she breathed, shifting uncomfortably.

"Don't worry," he reassured her, his voice soothing yet laced with desire. "No one's here to enjoy the view—it's just for me." He leaned closer, his hands sliding to her hips as he kissed the curve of her shoulder, his touch igniting every nerve.

"Jesse, we'll get in trouble if someone sees us," she pleaded, her voice trembling as he tucked himself under her hair, gently nipping at her earlobe.

"I could make love to you right here, on this chair, and no one would say a thing," he replied, his hands tugging her skirt back into place. His restraint only made the tension between them more unbearable. "I know that when you step into the club, all you crave is this—being here with me. You want my eyes to devour you, my desire wrapped around you, my hands claiming every inch of you," he whispered, each word sending an uncontrollable wave of heat crashing through her body.

"You can't keep pushing the boundaries a little more each time," she said, her voice shaky.

He smirked, his confidence unshaken. "Think so? Are you free on Sunday?"

"You're really persistent," she said, her gaze darting away as her resolve weakened.

"You haven't seen anything yet."

"Don't insist," she said, but the conviction in her words faltered.

"Look me in the eyes and tell me you don't want to see me outside of here."

Talie hesitated, her heart pounding as she met his gaze. His eyes were relentless, burning through every wall she tried to put up. She was trapped in the moment, unable to escape the pull between them.

"What do you want, Talie?" he asked, his mouth hovering just inches from hers.

"I can't," she sighed.

"What do you want?" he repeated, his lips brushing hers in the faintest of touches.

A powerful shiver shot through her body, and deep down, she longed for him to cross the line, to consume her and make her forget everything. But instead, he pulled back, his eyes still locked on her, taking in her parted lips, her trembling breath.

"Sunday afternoon, around three o'clock, I'll be at Mont-Royal Park, by the statue on Park Avenue," he murmured, his voice full of promise.

Her breath faltered as she pressed her lips together, meeting his gaze. Her heart screamed at her to say yes, but her mind—always practical, always guarded—fought back. "You're wasting your time," she whispered, forcing the words out.

Jesse's lips curved into a confident smile, unshaken. "My patience knows no bounds."

As he walked away, the air between them seemed to crackle, and Talie felt the undeniable ache of his absence. She escaped to the bathroom, where the large black velvet curtain at the entrance felt like a barrier between her and the world. She leaned against the cold sink, her fingers gripping the porcelain edge, her reflection in the mirror revealing the glimmer of conflict in her green eyes. *Memories are the most valuable things we hold in our hearts...* Rebecca's words echoed in her mind, a sharp contrast to the fear that whispered against her resolve.

She closed her eyes, exhaling shakily. What was she so afraid of? Being vulnerable? Getting hurt? Or perhaps what scared her most was how much she wanted to surrender.

Emerging from the bathroom, her gaze instinctively sought him out. He stood near his dressing room, casually tousling his hair, his easy smile aimed at a client. When his eyes found hers, his face broke into that dazzling smile—the one that made her heart flutter and ignited a flicker of hope within her that she couldn't suppress. In that instant, she knew her decision was already made, even if her mind hadn't caught up yet.

"How was it this time?" Rebecca asked, her eyes shimmering with curiosity as Talie returned from the bathroom.

"Intense."

Rebecca's eyebrows shot up, intrigued. "Really?"

Talie hesitated, her fingers fidgeting with the edge of her napkin. "He asked me to meet him at Mont-Royal Park on Sunday."

Rebecca's eyes widened. "Seriously? And what did you say?"

"I told him to let it go." The words felt hollow as she said them, doubt trailing behind them like a shadow.

Rebecca sighed, reaching over to give her a reassuring squeeze on the hand. "Maybe, for once, just listen to your heart."

Talie remained quiet, the conflict in her chest weighing her down like an anchor. She knew her friend was right. But what if following her heart led her straight into the kind of pain she wasn't sure she could recover from?

As the hours passed, the two friends decided to call it a night. Talie gathered her things, her nerves still frayed from the conversation with Jesse. Rebecca, ever the flirt, exchanged a lingering smile with Clayton as they passed him by, but Talie's focus remained locked on the man who had consumed her thoughts all night.

Jesse stepped into her path, his presence commanding her attention as if the universe had conspired to bring him closer. His hands found her waist, their warmth spreading through her like a slow burn. "Leaving already?"

"Yes," she said, her voice barely steady.

He leaned in, his lips grazing her cheek in a kiss that lingered just a fraction too long, the touch against her skin making her heart race. "See you on Sunday," she whispered, the words escaping her lips without conscious thought, as if they had a life of their own.

Jesse's grin widened, his blue eyes glittering with unmistakable satisfaction. "Sunday," he echoed, his voice full of quiet promise before he pulled away, disappearing into the crowd.

Rebecca, who had been watching from a few steps away, immediately turned to Talie, her expression a mix of disbelief and amusement. "I just can't believe it. I think this is the first time you've ever actually listened to me!"

Talie shot her a sideways glance, raising a skeptical brow. "Listened to you? Pretty sure I made that decision all on my own."

"I'm so excited for you! This is your first date in, what, two years?" Rebecca's enthusiasm was infectious, her eyes dancing with joy.

"I know. But this is… different."

Anxiety wove its way through her chest, mingling with the excitement she couldn't quite ignore. The thought of spending time with Jesse outside the safety of the club terrified her in ways she couldn't fully explain.

Rebecca leaned in, her grin devilish. "Out in the fresh air. Let's hope for sunshine. By the way, did you get a wax recently?"

"Becca!" Talie gasped, her cheeks flushing crimson.

"What?" she laughed, shrugging with exaggerated innocence. "A girl's got to be prepared for anything…"

"You're going to kill me," she groaned, shaking her head. "And for the record, there's no way I'm ending up in his bed on the first date."

"Who said you need a bed?" Rebecca's eyes sparkled with mischief. "If you only knew how many perfect, hidden spots there are at Mount Royal Park."

"Spare me the details, okay?" She couldn't help but smile. "I'm sure you've tested them all."

"Promise me you'll call as soon as you get home? I want *every* juicy detail!"

"Do I ever give you juicy details?"

"A girl can dream."

Talie had barely drifted into a fitful sleep when her alarm jolted her awake, its piercing ring shattering the fragile silence of the early morning. She groaned softly, the haze of her restless dreams clinging to her like a heavy fog as she stumbled into the kitchen. Her hands worked mechanically, slicing through vibrant oranges and pressing the juice into a glass. The bright tang of citrus filled the room, momentarily clearing the fog in her mind. But even the sharp, fresh scent couldn't quell the nervous energy simmering beneath her skin.

With the glass in hand, she stepped out onto her balcony, letting the morning air wrap around her. *It's still warm for September*, she thought. The sun kissed her face, golden and forgiving, as she closed her eyes and let her thoughts wander. For a moment, the world stilled. She breathed deeply, savoring the calm like a fragile gift.

But the peace was short-lived. The thought of her upcoming meeting with Jesse shattered the moment, sending her heart racing. It wasn't just a date. It was the possibility of something more, something intimate, something that both thrilled and terrified her. Her stomach fluttered with nervous energy she hadn't felt in years, and no amount of fresh air could temper it.

Back inside, she stepped into the shower, letting the warm water cascade over her. Her hands moved over her skin almost absentmindedly, tracing familiar curves that now seemed foreign under the weight of her thoughts. It had been over two years since anyone had touched her intimately, and the prospect of breaking that silence with Jesse made her pulse quicken.

She closed her eyes, the steam enveloping her, but it didn't stop the self-doubt creeping in. *What if he doesn't find me attractive?* she thought, her mind betraying the confidence she had worked so hard to build. She knew her figure was toned and athletic, a result of countless hours spent running and working out. Yet, the thought of baring not just her body but also her vulnerabilities to someone like Jesse felt daunting. Would he see her as enough—or would she end up another fleeting memory in his world?

Wrapping herself in a soft robe, she moved to the couch, curling her legs beneath her. Her gaze fell on the coffee table, where a book sat, its cover displaying a young couple walking hand in hand down a path that seemed to lead to paradise.

Four

Talie's steps quickened as she strolled down Mont-Royal Avenue, her thoughts swirling with unease. *I hope this doesn't turn into a series of awkward silences,* she thought, her fingers nervously smoothing the fabric of her trendy pink dress.

Passing a bustling restaurant terrace, she couldn't ignore the stares trailing her. A group of men, relaxed in the sun with beers in hand, exchanged appreciative looks.

"Want to join us for a drink?" one called out, his voice warm and bold.

"How about giving me your number?" another added with a playful grin.

She offered a polite smile, shaking her head as she moved past them. Their attention didn't unsettle her; it was what lay ahead that sent her heart racing. By the time she reached Park Avenue, the knot in her chest had tightened, her breath turning uneven with self-doubt creeping in. *What am I even doing? I'm not looking for a one-night stand, and a man like Jesse—who could have anyone he wanted—is probably just looking for another conquest.*

She slowed her steps, lowering her head as the crowd swirled around her. Her thoughts spiraled. *Maybe I'm just a challenge to him. A game. Nothing more.* She hesitated, the urge to turn back bubbling up inside her. *What if I'm just setting myself up to get hurt?*

Spinning on her heel, ready to retreat, she collided with someone. Strong hands steadied her as she stumbled slightly. Startled, she looked up, an apology on her lips— only to find herself staring into the very eyes she had been both longing for and dreading.

The bustling sounds of the city, the rhythmic shuffle of strangers' footsteps, even her own racing thoughts—all faded into nothingness. All that remained was him. His eyes, those impossibly blue eyes, seemed to catch the very light of the day, glowing as if they held the entire sky within them. Each glance was a pull, a magnetic force that tugged at her, deeper and deeper. The messy waves of his blonde hair shimmered under the sun, catching the light like strands of gold, while the stubble on his jawline framed the sharp perfection of his features, adding an edge that made her heart flutter. Every detail, every angle, every shadow was more striking in this moment, as if the universe had conspired to make him even more breathtaking.

Jesse's lips curved into an easy smile. "Where are you going in such a hurry?" he asked, his tone light, playful.

"I… I don't know," she stammered, her cheeks flushing.

His voice carried a warmth that resonated deep within her, wrapping around her like a quiet embrace. "I'm glad you're here."

Avoiding his gaze, she managed a response that concealed the nervous edge in her voice. "I'm glad, too."

They crossed the street together, stepping into the park's canopy of trees. Jesse paused to check his phone, giving her a moment to study him more closely. His casual jeans and fitted short-sleeve shirt hugged his broad frame, the fabric stretching slightly across his chest with every movement. Her gaze lingered on the way the sunlight danced on his tanned skin, her pulse quickening as her thoughts drifted into dangerous territory.

"You're not wearing your snake bracelet?" she remarked, breaking the comfortable silence.

"I only wear it at work," he said with a chuckle, slipping his phone back into his pocket.

As they started walking, she glanced over at him, curiosity flickering in her eyes. "How long have you been at Club Viator?"

"A little over ten years now."

"And you're not bored?" she pressed, raising an eyebrow.

"Bored? Never." His grin returned, disarming and full of mischief. "The clients are always smiling, always having a good time. What could be better than that?"

"Don't you feel, um, exploited?" she hesitated, unsure how to phrase her question. Her words felt clumsy, but she couldn't stop herself from asking.

He stopped walking, turning to face her fully. His expression softened, but the confidence in his gaze didn't waver. "Exploited? No. I'm not selling my body, Talie. I'm offering people an escape, a little joy, a little fantasy."

Her breath hitched as he reached for her hand, his fingers brushing hers in a gesture that was tender. "And what about you? How long have you been working in tourism?"

"About ten years," she said, her voice gaining steadiness, though her pulse continued to race under his scrutiny.

"And what led you to Club Viator?" he asked, his eyes glinting with curiosity.

She let out a soft laugh, the tension easing just slightly. "Rebecca," she admitted. "She kept going on and on about it. After a year of her nagging, I finally gave in."

"I'll have to thank her," he said. The intensity in his eyes made her cheeks flush, and she turned her head, focusing on the trees that lined their path. Anything to escape the spell he seemed to cast with just one look.

As her eyes drifted over the people they passed, she couldn't help but notice how many of them were staring at Jesse. Their gazes lingered on him—some curious, others admiring. She wondered if he even noticed. If it bothered him. But Jesse seemed oblivious, his focus fully on her and the tranquil beauty of the park surrounding them.

"Do clients ever recognize you outside of work?" she asked.

"Sometimes," he admitted with a casual shrug. "But they're usually discreet."

"Maybe they're embarrassed," she said, her voice tinged with hesitation. "No disrespect to what you do, but I don't exactly brag about being a regular at the club. I mean, I don't judge girls who go for a birthday or special events, but for those of us who go regularly… it feels a bit pathetic. Myself included."

Jesse didn't interrupt. He let her words linger, his silence encouraging her to keep going.

"There's something unhealthy about it all," she continued, her gaze falling to the ground. "Some of the girls… they'd sell their souls to the Devil just to spend one night with you."

"Did you sell yours to be here today?"

"Not yet," she replied, her lips curving into a faint smile as her thoughts drifted elsewhere.

"To find happiness, people often fall back on compulsions," he said, his tone shifting to something deeper, more reflective. "Some turn to drugs, alcohol, or gambling, while others seek solace in food, work, sports, or sex."

Talie blinked, surprised by his insight. She hadn't expected such a deep conversation with him. He seemed to peel back layers effortlessly.

"Hello, everyone. My name is Jesse Levine, and I'm into sex and sports," he quipped, mimicking an anonymous group introduction.

She laughed at his remark, but when she realized he was waiting for her to join in, she blushed. "I'm mostly into sports," she replied shyly.

"Anything else?" he pressed, his thumb lightly tracing the curve of her palm, igniting a warmth that spread through her like a slow-burning flame.

"Well..." she hesitated, her heart hammering in her chest. A faint smile tugged at her lips as she added, "Let's just say that a new interest has come up recently."

His grin widened, slow and knowing. "Interesting," he murmured, guiding her down a quieter path away from the crowd. "This way."

"You look like you know your way around."

"I do. I love coming here, it's relaxing. Have you been here before?"

Her thoughts drifted back to a time she wasn't sure she wanted to revisit. "My ex loved this place. We used to come here often. I haven't come back since."

Jesse's gaze sharpened, his curiosity deepening. "And what happened to this ex?"

Her chest tightened at the question. She hated talking about it—the memories still felt raw, like an old wound that hadn't quite healed. She felt a pang of shame, as if her ex's infidelity reflected some failure on her part. "He cheated on me," she said finally, the bitterness she tried to suppress slipping into her voice.

Jesse's expression softened, a flicker of understanding passing over his features. "Compulsive behavior," he said quietly, nodding as if he understood more than he let on.

"Through sex," she added, aiming for nonchalance, though the slight tremor in her voice betrayed her. "And you? Are you seeing anyone?"

His lips curved into a faint smile, but there was something guarded in his eyes. "I've been single since I started working at the club. I haven't really felt the need for a committed relationship," he said, his words measured.

Talie's heart clenched at his words. Stability was all she'd ever wanted—something she could count on, something real. But in one sentence, Jesse had revealed that commitment wasn't a priority for him. The excitement, the butterflies that had been fluttering in her chest moments ago, evaporated, leaving a hollow ache in their place. *Was this doomed from the start?* she wondered, the thought hitting her like a blow.

"Sometimes, against all odds, our needs change when we least expect it," he added, giving her hand a reassuring squeeze.

They walked in silence, the weight of his words hanging between them. The quiet should have felt awkward, but it didn't. It was charged, heavy with unspoken thoughts. When they finally reached Beaver Lake, Talie's breath caught. The landscape, bathed in golden sunlight, was more beautiful than she remembered—a peaceful escape from the noise of her mind. Hand in hand with the man who made her heart race, she stepped onto the lush green hillside. "I didn't remember it being this beautiful," she whispered, slipping off her sandals to feel the cool, soft grass beneath her feet.

Jesse's eyes never left her. He watched as she gathered her hair into a loose bun, exposing the graceful curve of her neck. The sight was almost too tempting. Stepping closer, he leaned in, his breath brushing against her exposed neck. "You're beautiful," he whispered.

The quiet intimacy of his voice sent a rush of warmth through her, and she felt her cheeks flush. She closed her eyes, letting herself savor the moment. He had this way of making her lose all sense of control, no matter where they were.

"I can't believe you agreed to see me outside the club," he said, breaking the silence as she turned to face him.

She lowered herself onto the grass, letting the cool blades brush against her palms, her gaze lifting to meet his. "Curiosity."

"Why now, after I've been asking for weeks?" he pressed, leaning in just close enough that his voice wrapped around her like a secret meant only for her ears.

Before she could answer, a familiar voice cut through the air, sharp and unexpected. "Talie?"

Her body stiffened, the sound dragging her back to a reality she hadn't prepared for. Startled, she looked up, her breath hitching as her heart kicked into overdrive. "Gabriel?" she stammered, barely masking the tremor in her voice.

"What a surprise!" he said, his gaze skimming over her before settling on Jesse. It wasn't casual—it was pointed, sharp, an unspoken challenge cloaked in his scrutiny.

As he sized him up, the silence between them thickened, humming with tension. The intensity of his stare made Talie's skin crawl, heat rising in her chest and spreading up her neck. She could feel the unasked questions hanging heavy in the air. Her discomfort swelled with every passing second, and she felt trapped, desperate to break the moment. Words spilled out before she could think. "This is Jesse."

Her voice was too quick, too abrupt, but it shattered the silence. Jesse remained calm, his demeanor an anchor against the storm that Gabriel's presence had unleashed. He met Gabriel's gaze with a polite nod, his expression unreadable, but the subtle shift of his body—closer to her—did not go unnoticed. His hand moved almost casually to her thigh, his touch light yet undeniable, as if silently declaring his place beside her.

Gabriel's eyes darted to Jesse's hand, his jaw tightening almost imperceptibly before he looked back at Talie. "Do you still come here often?" he asked, his tone clipped, dismissing Jesse entirely from the conversation.

"Not really," she replied, forcing her voice to remain steady as unease bubbled beneath the surface.

The silence that followed was suffocating, every second stretching unbearably. Finally, Gabriel shifted, shoving his hands into his pockets. "Well," he said, his forced smile not quite reaching his eyes, "I'll leave you to it." His eyes lingered on her one last time before he turned and walked away, his footsteps heavy with reluctance.

As soon as he disappeared, Talie exhaled, the tension in her shoulders unwinding like a coiled spring finally released. She hadn't even realized how tightly she'd been holding herself until he was gone. Jesse's hand rested lightly on her thigh, a small gesture of comfort that she was grateful for, even if she couldn't shake the unease left by Gabriel's sudden appearance.

"Unexpected encounter?" Jesse asked, noticing the shift in her mood.

She nodded, her eyes fixed on the lake's shimmering surface. "One I could've done without."

Jesse watched her closely, his brow furrowing as he studied her expression. "Is he the one who broke your heart?"

"Yes."

"Sunny Road agency?" Claudia answered the phone as her friends left her office.

"Now, spill the details!" Rebecca demanded playfully, heading toward the agency's cozy kitchen, the warm aroma of freshly brewed coffee filling the air.

Talie tried to suppress the grin tugging at her lips, but the memory of yesterday had her cheeks glowing. "It was… better than I expected."

Rebecca raised an eyebrow. "And?"

Talie rolled her eyes, already bracing for the inevitable. "No, Becca, I didn't sleep with him."

Her friend sighed dramatically, tossing her hands in the air. "Did he even try?"

"He invited me over for a drink at his place after our walk."

"And you didn't go?"

"No."

Rebecca slapped her forehead with theatrical flair. "I don't know whether to scream or stage an intervention. Are you seriously going to waste your life being afraid of taking a risk?"

Talie's smile faltered, her voice growing quieter. "Since he started at Club Viator, he's never had a serious relationship. Do you even want to guess how many women he's been with? Because I don't."

"Why not?" Rebecca countered, a wicked glint in her eye. "The more, the merrier. Sounds like he's well-qualified to deliver some unforgettable experiences."

Talie groaned, shaking her head. "Overqualified for someone who's only had two relationships." Her voice softened, her gaze dropping slightly as if lost in thought. "Speaking of relationships… I ran into Gabriel at the park. What are the odds?"

Rebecca's eyes widened in disbelief. "Gabriel? As in your ex?"

"Yes, Madame."

"And? What did he say?"

"Not much, really," Talie replied, the memory still fresh. "But seeing me with Jesse? I think it threw him off balance."

A grin spread across Rebecca's face as she clapped her hands together in delight. "Oh, I love this. Did Jesse know who he was?"

"Not at first. But he figured it out quickly enough," Talie said, a small smile tugging at her lips. "And let's just say… Jesse made sure Gabriel felt every bit of his presence."

"Oh my God! I wish I'd been there to see that!

"Yeah… 'uncomfortable' doesn't even begin to cover it. Jesse didn't even have to say a word. It was like his presence alone made Gabriel squirm."

"Sounds like he knows how to make an impression." She studied Talie closely, her eyes warm but curious. "So, are you going to see him again?"

Talie hesitated, her thoughts swirling. "I think, on some level, I agreed to see him yesterday because I wanted to prove something—to myself more than anyone else. I thought he'd be just another superficial, sex-driven guy. It would've made it easier to let go… to finally silence this obsession."

"But he turned out to be nothing like you expected, didn't he?"

Talie sighed deeply, running a hand through her hair. "Yeah… I'm so lost, Becca. My heart is pulling me one way, screaming yes, while my head is shouting just as loud that it's a bad idea."

Rebecca's lips curved into a gentle, encouraging smile, her eyes sparkling with warmth. "We only live once. If your heart's screaming yes, maybe it's time to listen."

They parted ways, heading back to their desks. Talie settled before her computer, her fingers poised above the keyboard, but the blank screen seemed to stare her down, demanding a focus she couldn't muster. Her mind wasn't in the present. It was stuck in the park, on the path she had walked with Jesse, tangled in the sound of his voice. She remembered asking him, almost cautiously. "Why did you decide to become an exotic dancer?"

He had paused for a moment, his expression thoughtful before answering. "When I was twenty-three, a good friend of mine worked at Club Viator. He was making good money and living this wild, free life with the clients. It sounded… exciting, so I joined him."

She'd noticed the hesitation in the way he'd drawn in a breath, the tension in the slight quirk of his brow. It was enough to tell her there had been more to the story, "And what happened to him?"

"In his last year at the club, he spiraled—drugs, alcohol, women… it all caught up to him," Jesse had admitted, his jaw tightening. "He lost control. Couldn't even perform anymore. After hours, he'd take clients to the private lounge, cross every line imaginable. The bosses gave him an ultimatum, but he didn't listen. He was fired, and everything unraveled. Locked himself away, stopped eating, shut the world out."

Jesse had exhaled as if letting out the weight of the story along with his breath. "The police had to break into his apartment. That's when they sent him to Philippe-Pinel Psychiatric Hospital."

"That's… horrible," she'd whispered.

"I visited him two years ago. They had him on so many meds he didn't even recognize me. It's like… the shell of him is there, but nothing's left inside," he had said, his voice thick with emotion.

She had reached out to touch his arm, offering silent comfort, even though she knew words wouldn't be enough.

Her thoughts were interrupted when Rebecca poked her head into the office. "Is your trip to Cancún all set?"

Talie blinked, the vivid memories of her walk with Jesse fading as reality pulled her back. "Almost. But I haven't done this tour in years. I'm nervous. Marc used to handle it, and now they've added the Ek Balam archaeological site to the itinerary since I was there last."

Rebecca stepped inside, leaning casually against the edge of Talie's desk. "You're going to be amazing, as always," she said, her voice reassuring. Then, her lips curled into a teasing grin. "But let's get to the important question. Do you think you can survive an entire week without Jesse?"

Talie laughed, rolling her eyes. "I'll be craving my dose the moment I get back," she said, mimicking an injection into her arm.

"Oh, I'm sure he'll be more than happy to give it to you."

The plane ascended smoothly into the crisp morning sky, the hum of the engines masking the low murmur of voices in the cabin. A minor delay earlier had frayed the patience of a few passengers, but Talie had diffused the tension with her easy charm, coaxing smiles and chuckles that softened the edges of their frustration. Now, as the city below faded into a blur of clouds, she finally allowed herself to exhale. Her gaze lingered on the horizon, but her mind drifted somewhere entirely different. Jesse.

By the time the plane touched down in Cancún, she had already switched gears, throwing herself fully into the week ahead. Her group was energetic, curious, and refreshingly easy to lead. They moved together through the stunning landscapes and ancient ruins of Chichen Itza, Tulum, Coba, Ek Balam, and Cozumel. With every stop, she painted vivid stories of history and culture, her lively humor drawing laughter and nods of approval from the crowd. But somewhere in the spaces between—on the bus rides, in the quiet moments when her gaze wandered over a scenic overlook—Jesse's shadow crept in. His touch, the heat of his breath on her neck, the way his presence seemed to overpower even the air between them. The memories felt so present, so tangible, it was almost maddening.

On their last evening, she joined a small group from the tour at a cozy local nightclub. Latin music filled the air as couples formed and dissolved on the dance floor. But even with the lively atmosphere surrounding her, all she could think about was how many hours remained before she'd be back home… and back in Jesse's world of irresistible seduction.

"It is currently 11:07 PM local time in Montreal, and the temperature is 15 degrees Celsius," the pilot announced as the plane touched down. Talie gazed out the window, her heart lifting at the sight of the illuminated airport. After a whirlwind week in Mexico, the familiar glow of home felt like a warm embrace.

By the time she finally stepped into her apartment, the clock was inching toward 1 AM. She dropped her suitcase by the door, kicked off her sandals, and sank into the couch. As her muscles relaxed, she reached for her phone out of habit—and froze when Jesse's name appeared on the missed calls list. Her breath caught as she played his message: "Hi, Talie, it's Jesse. I wanted to hear from you. Call me back." A rush of heat crept up her neck. She replayed the message once, twice, unable to resist the way it made her heart race. She set the phone down, pacing the room with anticipation tightening in her chest.

Morning came too quickly, yet she woke with an unexpected energy. The memories of Mexico, the lingering heat of the sun, and the thought of Jesse seemed to infuse her with vitality. She stepped into the agency, her voice light and cheerful. "Hey, girls!"

Rebecca was the first to spot her, letting out an excited squeal. "My girl is back!" She rushed over to envelop Talie in a hug, squeezing tightly.

"Wow, Miss Hawaiian Tropic!" Claudia added, her gaze sweeping over Talie's sun-kissed skin. "Look at that tan!"

"So, how was it? Tell us everything!" Rebecca asked, giving her a playful head-to-toe once-over.

"The group was fantastic, the visits to the archaeological sites were a success, and the weather couldn't have been better—it was perfect."

"And? You're not too exhausted from all that guiding and sunshine?"

"Not at all. Actually, I'm feeling great. Did you hit the club while I was gone?"

"We were saving it for your return," her friend said with a playful grin.

"Well, I'm back now!"

Five

"Now *that's* how you kick off a night!" Rebecca nudged her friends, watching Jesse command the stage with effortless charisma, drawing every gaze in the room.

Talie found her seat, her eyes fixed on him as he delivered a spectacular performance. But this time, it wasn't just his magnetism that held her captive. It was the depth she now recognized beneath it, the quiet intensity behind his charm, and it made him even harder to resist. *I hope he doesn't take too long to come over*, she thought, anticipation coiling inside her.

Clayton sauntered up to their table, a playful smirk tugging at his lips. "Ladies," he greeted, his gaze flicking to Rebecca.

"Let's get this party started," she announced, rattling off a borderline excessive order.

With a chuckle, he disappeared behind the bar, only to return moments later, balancing a tray loaded with colorful cocktails and shot glasses.

"This one's for you," she said, handing him a shot, her signature flirtatious grin in place.

"Cheers!" Claudia raised her glass, and the others quickly followed suit. In perfect sync, they downed their shots.

A sharp burn seared Talie's throat, making her cringe. "Ugh, I hate this shooter."

Rebecca laughed, raising an eyebrow. "Snakebite. It lives up to its name." Her eyes slid back to Clayton, her lips curling mischievously as she licked the remnants of the alcohol off them.

He leaned down, brushing his lips near her ear. "If you're up for it, I'd love to have you over for a drink at my place tonight," he murmured, his voice low and inviting.

Rebecca flashed him a stunning smile and leaned closer. "I hope you'll keep me for more than just a drink," she hinted, her fingers lightly trailing down his back.

"Definitely," he said with a nod before stepping away, leaving them to their drinks.

Rebecca turned back to Talie and Claudia, raising her glass high. "Tonight, we're celebrating!" she declared, her voice bright and brimming with excitement.

Talie let out a soft laugh, but her mind was already elsewhere. Her eyes wandered back to the bar, searching for Jesse. She spotted him with a client, collecting some money before he disappeared into the private lounge. *How much longer?* she wondered, feeling impatience stir inside her. It wasn't like her to be this restless.

Just then, Tristan approached their table, his gaze settling on Claudia. "Good evening."

Claudia smiled, slipping a bill into his hand. Without missing a beat, he leaned in close. "Come with me," he whispered. With a wink at her friends, she followed him into the private lounge.

"She must be his best customer," Rebecca commented with a smirk.

"Don't exaggerate," Talie countered. "She only gets one or two dances a week."

Rebecca raised an eyebrow. "Maybe, but have you noticed he doesn't do many private dances for anyone else? That says something."

Talie's gaze swept the room again, scanning for Jesse. After a few moments, the private lounge door swung open, and there he was. Her eyes locked onto him, following his every step with an anticipation she couldn't suppress. She silently willed him to look her way and break the monotony that had begun to settle. But instead, he headed to the bar, grabbed a bottle of water, and struck up a conversation with Clayton.

"Tonight, I'm finally going to have sex with Clayton," Rebecca declared, clinking her glass against Talie's with a wicked smirk.

Talie blinked, caught off guard. "What are you talking about?"

"He invited me over for a drink after the club closes!"

"You must be thrilled!" she said, pushing aside the empty glasses cluttering their table, forcing herself to keep her focus on Rebecca.

But no matter how hard she tried, her resolve wavered. Her attention slipped. And before she could stop herself, her gaze drifted—pulled by an invisible force—back to the bar. The air in her lungs stilled as their eyes met, the moment stretching between them, taut and charged. A slow, knowing smile played on his lips, the kind that made it clear he knew exactly the effect he had on her. Setting down his water bottle, he moved toward her, his strides purposeful yet unhurried. When he finally reached her, he leaned in just enough for his voice to blend into the intimate noise around them. "Is there something special going on tonight?"

"Looks like it," she replied, searching for that familiar spark in his eyes that always drew her in.

"And what are we celebrating? Your long break from the club?" he teased.

"I was guiding a tour group in Cancún."

"Ah, that explains the gorgeous tan," he said, his gaze sweeping over her.

When it lingered on her thighs, barely concealed by her white dress, something in his expression darkened—smoldering, charged. Slowly, his tongue swept over his lower lip, the unconscious gesture igniting a shiver deep within her.

Another dancer approached, interrupting the moment. Jesse exchanged a few quick words, his demeanor all business, before turning back to her. "Wait for me," he said, brushing her arm lightly before walking away.

Talie exhaled, turning back to her friend. "I think I should stop drinking."

"Why? The night's just getting started," she replied, raising an eyebrow.

"If I keep this up, I might end up saying more than I intend to…"

"And?"

"Let's just agree that now's not the time or place for that conversation."

Rebecca laughed and pushed another drink toward her friend. "You could always use this as an opportunity to tell him a few things you've been holding back…"

"I'm already losing my composure thanks to your Snakebite," she said, eyeing the drink with suspicion.

"Oh, come on! Just one more!"

Talie sighed, raising her glass. "I'm holding you responsible for the rest of the night."

Rebecca grinned, unfazed, and promptly ordered another round while Clayton hovered nearby, clearing the table. With a slow, deliberate tug, she adjusted her low-cut top, revealing just a hint more cleavage. His gaze flickered downward, lingering on the newly exposed skin before he flashed her a promising smile.

"Becca, how do you manage to drink so much?" Talie asked, leaning back with mock exasperation.

"It's just a habit, girl!"

"I'd hate to see the state of your liver," she quipped, shaking her head.

Rebecca shrugged, unbothered. "Not me."

Claudia rejoined them, radiating smug satisfaction. "That was something, girls."

"Tell us everything!" Rebecca leaning in, eyes bright with excitement.

"There was no one else in the room, and Tristan didn't waste any time. His hands were everywhere!"

"Woooo!" Rebecca chimed, her eyes widening.

"And I made sure to enjoy every second of it."

Talie listened, a dreamy expression crossing her features as she pictured herself in the private lounge, her self-control hanging by a thread. Lost in her desires, she barely noticed when her friends suddenly fell silent. "Girls," she said, breaking free from her thoughts. "Tonight, if I get the chance, I'm making a move on Jesse."

Rebecca and Claudia's eyes widened in synchronized alarm, hands shooting up in a silent plea for her to stop. But Talie, oblivious, let her words slip out before she fully processed them. "If he takes me to the private lounge, my hands might start wandering too."

"Shh," Claudia's sharp whisper sliced through the air, her eyes flicking past Talie's shoulder with a silent warning.

Beside her, Rebecca pressed her lips together, fighting back a laugh.

Talie's stomach twisted as unease crept over her, cold and undeniable. Slowly, realization sank in—something was off. Her heart lurched, and she didn't dare turn around. Jesse was standing right there, having overheard every mortifying word. The warmth of his hand settling on her shoulder confirmed her worst fear.

"I was just coming to get you," he said softly, amusement threading through his tone.

Flashing a sheepish, tipsy grin at her friends, Talie pushed to her feet a little too fast. The world tilted, her balance wavering—until Jesse's steady hand found hers, anchoring her. She held onto him, his firm grip leading her toward the private area. By the time they reached the secluded space, she all but collapsed into the chair, exhaling sharply.

"It's been quite the night," Jesse said with a smile.

Talie's vision blurred from the alcohol, but she still noticed the way he moved closer, each step slow and tantalizing.

"Any special requests after being away for so long?" he asked, his voice low, filled with suggestion.

"I'm not sure," she mumbled, her fingers tracing the gold snake bracelet coiled around his arm.

He slipped it off, letting it dangle between his fingers before meeting her gaze, "You like it?"

"It's very sexy," she said while he slid the bracelet up her arm, adjusting it to fit snugly around her bicep.

"I'll give it to you if you let me…"

"If I let you…" she tried to say, her voice trailing off while her vision continued to blur.

He crouched beside her, the space between them vanishing, his breath teasing her skin. "…if you let me take possession of your body and soul," he murmured, his lips ghosting along her neck.

A soft sigh slipped from her lips, and she leaned back, instinctively yielding to his touch. His mouth followed, pressing slow, lingering kisses along her skin, each one leaving a trail of heat in its wake.

"I heard you wanted to get wild with me," he whispered, his lips grazing her shoulder. He caught the delicate strap of her dress between his teeth, slowly pulling it down her arm as he moved between her legs. "Your skin is so soft, so warm," he breathed, his voice thick with desire.

His hands found hers, guiding them to the firm, sculpted lines of his chest. She hesitated for a moment before letting her fingers explore him, feeling the heat and power beneath his skin.

Jesse's gaze darkened with raw desire, his touch growing bolder, roaming over her body with increasing need. "You still haven't told me what you want tonight."

"I don't know," she whispered, her voice almost inaudible, barely able to speak under the intensity of the moment.

"I think I know," he breathed, slipping his hand beneath her skirt. He teased her, inching closer with every touch, his hand lighting a fire deep within her.

Lost in the rhythm of his mouth and the skilled dance of his hands, Talie barely registered the door to the private lounge creaking open. A dancer entered with a client, but she was too immersed in the flood of sensations Jesse was stirring within her to care.

Then, through the haze of pleasure, a faint voice—distant, like it was from another realm—called her name. With great effort, she forced her eyes open and found Jesse gazing at her.

"Come on," he said softly, his voice a lifeline pulling her back to reality. "I'll help you back to the club."

"Is it over?" she murmured, still confused, struggling to gather her bearings.

He chuckled, flashing one of his most dazzling smiles. "Yeah, beautiful. I'm so skilled, you fell asleep while I was caressing you."

With her vision still blurry, she tried to focus on his face as he offered his hand to help her up. "I feel so drunk," she giggled, the sound light and carefree. "I don't know how I'm going to make it back to my place."

"Don't worry," he murmured, amusement and affection dancing in his eyes. "I've got you."

As he guided her back, the world spun around her, but his strong arm wrapped firmly around her waist kept her anchored. The warmth of his body against hers and the steady rhythm of his steps made everything seem a little less chaotic. By the time they reached the table, her friends were already in fits of laughter at her flushed face and glassy eyes. Talie collapsed into her chair, resting her chin in the palm of her hand with a defeated sigh.

"See you later, gorgeous," Jesse whispered before he walked away.

"Ugh. I'm so wasted," Talie groaned.

"That's exactly what it looks like, girl," Rebecca said with a chuckle.

"I actually fell asleep with his hands all over me," she slurred, embarrassment and disbelief in her voice.

Her friends erupted into laughter, their giggles filling the air around them. Talie's flushed expression only made the moment more hilarious.

"I feel awful," she muttered, frustrated by how easily her friends were enjoying themselves while she could barely stay upright. "How do you two drink this much and still manage to walk straight?"

"I'll probably slow down if I want to enjoy what's coming next," Rebecca replied, her eyes twinkling mischievously.

"Hey, it's Tristan's turn!" Claudia shouted, bouncing in her seat with such enthusiasm that her breasts nearly popped out of her overly tight top.

Rebecca immediately mirrored Claudia's excitement, swaying her hips dramatically and chanting, "Tristan, Tristan!" in an exaggerated, sultry voice. Nearby customers turned to watch, but Rebecca didn't care, fully caught up in the moment. "Maybe you should make him an indecent proposal to heat things up tonight," she teased, winking at Claudia.

"Oh, absolutely!" Claudia agreed, her eyes lighting up. Then she turned to Talie, a grin spreading across her face. "Looks like you'll be the only one left, girl! Don't you want to pick up where you and Jesse left off earlier?"

"Nah, too risky," she replied, shaking her head.

Claudia playfully slapped Talie's thigh, her eyes gleaming while Jesse took the stage with Tristan. "Now that's the kind of danger I wouldn't mind falling into."

Talie grinned at her friends, her gaze inevitably drawn back to Jesse's athletic, sensual form moving on stage. For a moment, she was completely lost in the memory of their heated encounter in the private lounge, the way his fingers had trailed over her skin. The details were a little hazy, blurred by the alcohol, but she knew that reality would hit her hard the next morning.

"Mmm, I bet you'd love to go back to that private lounge," Claudia teased, snapping her out of her thoughts.

"Look at those tight, muscular cheeks! Now turn around—let's see what else you're working with!" Rebecca chimed in, her gaze dripping with playful lust.

Biting back her giggles, Talie forced herself to focus on Jesse's performance, watching him finish before vanishing into the crowd. "Good thing I love you girls," she murmured, both amused and a little overwhelmed by their antics.

"We love you too!" Rebecca said, pulling Talie into a tight, affectionate hug.

Comforted by her friend's warmth, she closed her eyes, savoring the brief moment of calm, until Jesse's voice cut through, almost like a dream. "Who's driving tonight?"

Rebecca glanced at Talie, amused. "It was supposed to be her."

Talie blinked up at Jesse, her gaze locking onto his piercing blue eyes. "We've all had a little too much to drink," she admitted, her hair falling into her face as she smiled sheepishly.

Jesse reached out, his fingertips tracing a slow path along her cheek before tucking a stray strand of hair behind her ear. "I've never seen you like this before."

"It's been a while since I let myself."

"Did you call a taxi?" he asked, his concern hidden behind the smile that tugged at his lips.

"Rebecca's got a date with Clayton after closing," she explained, her words slurring slightly. "He'll make sure we get home safely."

Jesse leaned in, his breath warm against her ear. "Or… I could take you home," he whispered, his voice low, the suggestion thick with promise.

Talie's heart raced, and when her eyes locked with his, all rational thought evaporated. Whether it was the alcohol or the magnetic pull she felt toward him, Jesse seemed even more irresistible than usual. His smile was dazzling, his white teeth gleaming, and all she could think about was tasting those lips, feeling his touch again. "Okay," she murmured, the decision coming almost automatically.

"Perfect," Jesse said, his hand brushing her thigh before he slipped away.

When she turned back to her table, the energy shifted. Rebecca and Claudia's glances were anything but subtle. "He's going to take me home," Talie whispered, her heart still racing.

Rebecca's reaction was instant. "What?" she half-yelled, loud enough to turn a few heads.

"He offered, and I said yes."

"This carefree vibe suits you!" Claudia cheered, clinking her glass with Talie's.

Rebecca leaned in closer, her eyes sparkling with mischief. "You should get drunk more often."

Talie laughed softly, her smile faltering with a flicker of uncertainty. "We'll see how I feel in the morning."

The three friends decided to leave before the club closed, their spirits high after a night overflowing with laughter and playful chaos. Outside, the cool air hit them like a welcomed shock, refreshing and slightly sobering, though their tipsy giggles still filled the quiet streets.

"You should have seen your face when you came back from the private lounge," Claudia teased, her laughter infectious and bright.

Talie groaned dramatically. "Don't remind me! I swear I completely lost it in there more than once."

"An unforgettable night," Rebecca said while the crowd gradually thinned, leaving behind only a few lingering souls drifting out of the club.

The three of them stood together, fully aware that the men they were waiting for were the subject of countless whispered fantasies at Club Viator. Finally, Jesse and Clayton emerged, their confident strides cutting through the night like a scene perfectly cued. Flashing easy, knowing smiles, they approached the group, the unspoken electricity between them crackling in the cool air.

"Ready to go?" Jesse asked.

Talie pulled her friends into a final hug, holding on for a moment longer.

"Good night," Rebecca whispered in her ear. "Call me tomorrow?" she added with a sly wink.

Talie nodded, warmth lingering in her chest as she fell into step beside Jesse. As they walked, she couldn't help but notice the way his leather jacket draped over his broad shoulders, exuding effortless cool.

"Fun night," he teased, his gaze catching hers with an amused spark.

Her lips curved into a sheepish smile. "We were like teenagers who couldn't handle their alcohol."

"Maybe," he replied, his grin deepening in a way that sent a ripple of heat through her veins. "But I liked seeing that carefree side of you."

The words lingered between them, settling into the quiet rhythm of their footsteps. As they rounded the corner, the hush of the empty street gave way to the gleam of polished metal under the streetlights. Three sports cars stood waiting: a sleek black Porsche Boxster, a bold yellow Mitsubishi Eclipse, and a silver Maserati GranTurismo.

Talie's gaze flitted between them, her interest ignited. The Mitsubishi screamed for attention, too loud and too flashy. The Porsche, while elegant, felt predictable. But the Maserati—oh, that Maserati. Radiating pure class.

Jesse reached into his pocket, and with the press of a button, the Maserati's lights flickered to life. Talie couldn't stop the smile tugging at her lips. "Of course," she murmured under her breath, her voice soft but impressed. "I see why you've stuck around here for so long."

She slid into the luxurious interior, the soft red leather wrapping her in a comforting embrace. She stretched her legs out, sinking into the seat. "Wow," she whispered, already feeling the gentle pull of sleep.

Jesse's voice broke through her hazy thoughts, light and amused. "Too bad you can't drive right now. I'd have let you take the wheel."

Her head tilted slightly, eyes half-lidded, and a faint smile curved her lips. "I might have lost track of time tonight, but I won't forget that offer."

Jesse's laugh rumbled low, blending seamlessly with the deep growl of the engine coming to life. The sound vibrated through the cabin, smooth and thrilling, like the promise of a long-forgotten adventure. Outside, the night felt calm, the city's lights casting a soft glow over the empty streets as they cruised away.

"I would've thought a car like this would bring out a sportier driving style," she teased.

Jesse's grin widened, his fingers drummed lightly on the wheel. "Normally, it does," he admitted, his tone filled with playful restraint. "But I don't want you getting sick."

Talie turned her gaze toward the window, watching the city lights stretch into streaks of gold and white. The lights, the people, the cars—they all blurred by in dizzying patterns. Jesse was right. With the alcohol swirling inside her, a fast ride would have been too much for her stomach to handle.

"Are you coming to my place?" he asked, breaking the easy stillness that had settled between them.

She hesitated, her fingers brushing the edge of her seatbelt before she shook her head softly. "No. I'd rather you take me home. Drop me off on Masson, near Sixth Avenue. I think I need a little fresh air before I head in."

She let her eyes flutter closed for a moment, only opening them when the car rolled to a gentle stop. She exhaled, unbuckling her seatbelt with a soft click.

"I'll walk with you, if you don't mind. I'm not used to going straight to bed after work," he said, already stepping out of the car before she could refuse.

The street was quiet, save for the faint murmur of the city in the distance. Together, they strolled slowly, their footsteps rhythmic against the pavement. Talie's voice broke the quiet hum of the night. "What do you usually do after nights at the club?"

"Clayton and I grab a drink. We relax and talk."

"On those rare nights when you're not leaving with an interesting client," she added, casting him a teasing glance.

His lips curled into a slow, knowing smile. "Like you?"

Her grin faltered just a little. "Is that a regular thing? Taking girls home after closing?"

"No, not really. It doesn't happen often. Most of the guys are in relationships—performing is just a paycheck to them, nothing more. And the ones who do meet customers outside the club…" He paused, his gaze dragging over her like a slow caress. "They tend to be discreet about it."

As he spoke, his tongue swept across his lower lip, just a brief, unconscious movement. Her gaze caught on it before she could stop herself, drawn in by the effortless motion. A flush crept up her neck, heat sparking in her chest and spreading like a slow burn.

"I wouldn't have guessed that," she murmured, slowing her pace.

With his hands tucked casually into the pockets of his leather jacket, Jesse stopped in front of her, his gaze steady, unshaken. The streetlights caught in his eyes, making them shimmer with something irresistible. And that smile—breathtaking, so naturally perfect. Talie's pulse kicked up a notch, and for once, she let her heart take the lead over her head.

"Do you want to come up?" The words slipped out before she could second-guess herself.

Jesse paused, one brow lifting slightly. "You're not tired?"

"A little," she admitted, her voice softer now. "But my head's still spinning. I hate going to bed feeling dizzy."

His gaze held hers for a beat, searching, as if weighing her words. "Are you sure?"

"Yes," she said, the certainty of her voice catching her by surprise.

A slow smile spread across his face, lighting up his eyes with a warmth that curled deep in her chest. Without another word, he reached for her hand, his touch igniting sparks along her skin. They made their way up to her apartment, the quiet of the night amplifying the soft echo of their footsteps and the steady thud of her heart.

Inside, she eased the door shut behind them, the inviting hush of her apartment closing in around them like a secret.

"Make yourself comfortable," she said, already heading for the hallway. "I'll be right back."

Left alone, Jesse wandered into the living room, his fingers grazing the various trinkets and artifacts from her travels, each piece telling its own story. His gaze settled on an unusual musical instrument, its detailed carvings drawing him in with a silent invitation.

"Want something to drink?" Talie's voice interrupted his thoughts.

He looked up, and for a moment, his breath hitched. She stood framed in the doorway, her hair loosely swept back to reveal the soft curve of her neck. Something about the way she stood—casual yet radiant—held him completely captive.

"No, I'm good," he said, his tone low, carrying an edge he couldn't quite hide.

The slow drag of his gaze sent a flush of warmth up her spine. Needing a moment, she turned toward the kitchen, pretending to busy herself while questioning her decision to invite him up. She had envisioned light conversation, something easy, but the weight of their chemistry pressed in, thick and inescapable.

When she returned, Jesse was holding a small wooden flute, running his fingers over the intricate carvings.

"I picked that up in Thailand," she said, watching him study the piece with quiet curiosity.

"This is nice."

"You have to pull here while blowing," she said, stepping closer to demonstrate.

He raised an eyebrow, then gave it a try. A piercing screech erupted from the flute, shattering the room's stillness. Talie doubled over with laughter, and Jesse's deep chuckle soon followed, the tension between them unraveling in shared amusement.

Still grinning, he set the flute back on the shelf, his gaze sweeping the room before he sank into her couch. "Did you enjoy Cancún?" he asked, watching her move.

"Yeah. The weather was perfect," she replied, her mind momentarily drifting to sun-drenched beaches and salty air.

He tilted his head, his voice quieter now. "I wondered about your long absence."

She opened her mouth to answer but faltered as he reached for her hand. Before she could process the moment, he had guided her onto his lap, positioning her so they were face-to-face. Her breath hitched, the sudden closeness leaving no room for distraction or retreat. His hands found her hips, anchoring her there, the tips of his fingers grazing the curve of her thighs with an excruciating slowness.

"Jesse…" Her voice wavered, uncertainty threading through each syllable. "Tell me you don't do this with all your clients."

His expression softened, something unreadable flickering in his gaze. "I don't."

"But those women," she pressed, her voice quieter now, almost hesitant. "They're at the club every night… trying anything to get your attention."

Jesse exhaled, the edge of a smile playing on his lips. "A few months ago, you might've had a reason to question it." He paused, his thumb brushing gently over the curve of her hip, grounding her in the moment. "But not anymore."

Talie's heart thundered in her chest as she searched his face, craving more—craving him.

"Recently, I met a woman who's unlike anyone I've ever known. She's captivating, mysterious, impossible to resist. And she's the only one I want." His words landed like a confession, raw and unfiltered. "You're the only one I want."

Her heart pounded when his grip tightened on her hips, drawing her flush against him. She could feel his arousal through the thin barrier of her panties, hard and insistent, fueling the ache that pulsed low in her belly. Her back arched instinctively, her body attuned to the silent promise in his touch, every nerve thrumming with anticipation.

"I'll torment you until there's no doubt left," he whispered, his lips hovering just above hers, his words like velvet. "Until you feel it deep in your soul that you're the only one I want."

"I feel it," she breathed, her voice barely audible.

"I want you to feel it with a clear head," he said, the edge of desire still roughening his tone. "Without the haze of alcohol." His gaze lingered on her lips, his voice dropping to a husky murmur. "I want you to remember every second of our first time. Every touch, every gasp."

A slow, molten ache unfurled deep in Talie's core, his words stroking a fire that left her taut with longing. With deliberate care, he lifted her from his lap, his touch gentle despite the raw hunger she'd seen in his eyes just moments ago. As she settled onto the cushion beside him, her gaze flickered downward, drawn to the thick bulge straining against his jeans—a stark reminder of just how easily they could have unraveled.

Leaning close, his lips brushed her ear. "I have to go, but trust me, this is far from over." His lips lingered on the curve of her neck, leaving her skin aflame. "Call me," he whispered, his breath a final caress before he stepped back, leaving her wrapped in a haze of longing and anticipation.

The blaring alarm jolted Talie awake, yanking her from vivid dreams into the golden morning light spilling through her window. She stretched, a slow smile curling her lips as her thoughts drifted back to the electrifying night with Jesse. Butterflies stirred in her stomach, the memory of his whispered promises and lingering touch still seared into her skin. If he had stayed just a little longer, she knew they would have ended up tangled in her sheets.

Despite her fear of being just another notch on his bedpost, he had convinced her, if only for one night, that she was truly special. His decision to leave, rather than give in to their passion, left her both confused and intrigued.

Still battling the remnants of her hangover, she strolled into the agency later that morning. Her friends were already waiting, their faces lighting up with curiosity the moment they spotted her.

"I've got nothing to say," she said with a playful smile.

"Liar!" Claudia called out, trailing after her while she moved further inside.

"Jesse drove you home, and you expect us to believe that nothing happened?" Rebecca added.

Casting a sly glance their way, Talie smirked knowingly. "You know I don't spill personal details, girls. I'm not like Becca."

Rebecca's grin widened triumphantly. "Well, since you asked so nicely, I had an amazing night."

"Amazing enough for you to still remember it?" Talie raised an eyebrow.

"Oh, definitely," she replied, leaning in. "The man was in fantastic shape, and he exceeded all my expectations. Great sex, just the way I like it."

Talie laughed, shaking her head. "You never change, Becca."

"And you, Miss Mysterious?" Claudia pressed, her gaze gleaming with curiosity. "Any juicy details to share?"

The conversation paused, all eyes on Talie. "So?" they chimed in unison. "Did you sleep with him?"

She chuckled and shook her head in mock exasperation. "You're all so curious! No, I didn't sleep with him." Her friends exchanged skeptical glances, clearly unconvinced. In truth, if Jesse hadn't shown such remarkable self-control, her answer might have been different.

As she sank back into her desk chair, a sigh escaped her lips, her thoughts lingering on the emotions of the previous night rather than the mountain of work awaiting her. She pulled out her phone and turned it over in her hands, replaying the last message Jesse had left her.

"Talie, it's Jesse. If you're free tomorrow, call me. I want to see you in the daylight…"

The fluttering excitement he stirred within her was undeniable, but so was the familiar fear—fear of opening her heart only to have it shattered again.

Rebecca chose that moment to appear, sliding into the chair across from her with an air of casual curiosity. "So? Are you going to see him again?"

Talie rubbed her temples, dropping her phone onto the desk. "I'm exhausted, Becca."

"Physically or emotionally?"

"Both," she admitted, exhaling a sigh that carried more weight than she intended. "I don't know where this is going to lead…"

Rebecca's expression softened, a rare moment of seriousness settling in her voice. "Stop worrying and just enjoy the moment—right here, right now."

Talie nodded slowly, clinging to the simple truth of those words. *Here and now*, she repeated, as if grounding herself in the present could soften the uncertainty of the future.

That night, she lingered in the doorway of her apartment longer than usual. The silence of her home felt heavier than before, punctuated only by the faint hum of the city outside.

…Here and now. Rebecca's words echoed, more insistent this time.

She dropped her bag and headed for the couch, sinking into the cushions with her phone already in hand.

The screen glowed, Jesse's number hovering in her call history. For once, she didn't hesitate.

"Jesse, it's Talie. I'm free around two tomorrow. Call me back."

The line disconnected with a soft click, leaving her staring into the quiet stillness of her apartment. Settling into bed, the faint glow of the clock blinked in the dim light. She closed her eyes, her heartbeat a calm rhythm against the pillow. For the first time in months, the uncertainty didn't consume her. Her heart and mind, finally in harmony, brought her a fragile peace—one she hadn't felt in so long.

By choosing to see Jesse again, she was taking a risk. Yet tonight, that vulnerability didn't feel like a weakness. It felt like hope.

"Talie, come quick!" her friends shouted, their voices tinged with urgency.

Heart pounding, she rushed out of her office, bracing for the worst. But as soon as she reached the front of the agency, her panic melted into stunned disbelief. Jesse had just parked his Maserati outside, its sleek silver surface gleaming under the midday sun. A small crowd had already gathered, murmurs of curiosity spreading through the onlookers.

With his sunglasses resting low on his nose and a confident ease in his stride, he stepped out of the sports car like he owned the street. Talie's friends froze, their gazes following his every move, awe and intrigue painted across their faces.

A wave of fluttering anticipation tightened Talie's nerves. She quickly smoothed down her hair and tugged discreetly at her neckline, desperate for composure. Her pulse raced, every beat loud in her ears.

"I hope you're finally ready to drop those ridiculous principles about not dating a guy who strips for a living," Rebecca said, leaning in with a mischievous grin.

Before Talie could fire back, the glass door swung open, and Jesse stepped into the agency, his presence commanding the room like a well-rehearsed entrance. He pushed his sunglasses up onto his head, revealing the striking glint of his blue eyes before locking his gaze on Talie. "Busy day?" he asked, his tone laced with that familiar teasing edge.

Heat crawled up Talie's neck, her pulse hammering while she fought for a casual response. "Let's just say your car doesn't exactly blend in," she replied, hoping her voice didn't betray how flustered she felt. Of course, it wasn't the Maserati that had everyone buzzing—it was him.

Jesse's smile widened, slow and knowing, his eyes flicking to the trio watching unabashedly from near the window.

"Claudia, Rebecca, and Laurence," Talie said quickly, introducing her friends, who pretended to look busy even if they were practically leaning into the conversation.

"Always a pleasure to see familiar faces," he said, his voice a smooth caress. He nodded at each of them, his gaze lingering just long enough to make an impression.

The trio responded with quiet, appreciative smiles, while Talie fought to keep her reaction in check. He turned back to her, his posture relaxed, but his eyes carrying that playful gleam. "Want to show me around?"

"Sure," she agreed, leading him deeper into the office. The subtle buzz of whispers trailed behind them, her friends undoubtedly dissecting every glance, every step.

Jesse paused at her desk, his gaze sweeping over the towering stack of paperwork. He tilted his head, his brow lifting slightly. "Aren't you supposed to finish at two?"

She glanced at the clock, guilt flickering across her face. "I got a little caught up."

"Come on." His voice carried a low, coaxing charm as he turned toward the exit. "Let's get out of here."

She hesitated, already reaching for her bag. "Where are we going?"

He shrugged, a playful glint in his eyes, before stepping outside. As he passed Talie's friends, he offered a nod, his voice laced with mystery. "I guess we'll see."

Rebecca watched them with barely concealed glee. "Too bad he didn't come with Clayton. We could've made it a double date."

"So we can be your chaperones?" she called back, before trailing after Jesse.

Sliding into the passenger seat of the Maserati, she cast one last glance at the agency window. Her friends were still glued to the glass, their curious faces pressed against it like a scene from a comedy. Jesse started the engine with a grin, the growl of the car cutting through the afternoon calm and turning heads as they pulled away.

"I didn't expect to see you here," she said, settling into the luxurious leather seat.

"I wanted to surprise you," he said, the corner of his mouth lifting.

"Well, you definitely succeeded."

At an intersection, they stopped next to a sleek convertible Mercedes. Talie's eyes flicked toward the two stunning blondes inside, who were blatantly eyeing Jesse with interest. He responded with a polite, dismissive smile before turning his attention back to her. She kept her gaze forward, pretending not to notice—but a flicker of satisfaction danced through her when he sped off, leaving the Mercedes far behind.

"How's your hangover?" he asked, glancing over with a knowing smile.

"Pretty brutal," she admitted, letting out a groan. "I miss my twenties."

"But thirty is when women are truly beautiful," he said, quoting Ferland with a sincerity that warmed her.

Talie chuckled softly. "Have you always been this smooth, or is it something you picked up at the club?"

His laughter rang out, deep and unguarded. "I had some charm before Club Viator, but... let's just say it's been refined over the years."

The city blurred past the window, leaving Talie in silence. Thoughts swirled, doubt creeping in. Thirty, single, no kids... She wondered what Jesse wanted from life.

Could she picture him as a father? Could an exotic dancer make a good dad? Her heart raced, battling the doubts that had haunted her since meeting him. She wanted to trust him, but her past made it difficult. "When I was little, my parents called me 'the charmer'," he said, breaking the silence.

She looked over, a smile playing on her lips while picturing a younger version of him, mischief sparkling in those same blue eyes. "I bet you were adorable."

"I was very good at getting what I wanted," he replied, flashing her a knowing grin.

Laughter bubbled up in her chest, tension slipping away like smoke. It was his honesty—raw and effortless—that made her want to let her guard down, no matter how much it terrified her.

The city soon gave way to open fields, and the Maserati's tires crunched over a dirt road. Ahead, a picturesque country house appeared, nestled between rows of apple trees that stretched to the horizon. The distant mountains loomed like silent guardians.

"Here we are," Jesse announced, parking the car.

Talie stepped out, the cool country air wrapping around her. She took in the view, her breath catching. "It's beautiful," she whispered, her voice full of wonder.

Jesse reached for her hand, his fingers brushing against hers in a way that sent an all-too-familiar thrill through her. Together, they walked toward the house, where an elderly woman waited at the door, her face breaking into a radiant smile.

"Hello, my handsome boy," she said, kissing Jesse on both cheeks before turning her bright, kind gaze to Talie. Studying her for just a moment, the woman pulled her into a gentle hug.

"Grace, this is Talie," Jesse introduced.

"It's a pleasure to meet you," Talie said, taken aback by the woman's warmth.

"She's special," Grace remarked, giving Jesse a knowing look. "Take good care of her."

"I will," he promised, his voice low and sincere.

She turned her attention back to Talie, her expression soft but intense. "You've got a real treasure in your hands," she said. "You can trust him."

Jesse chuckled lightly, breaking the intensity. "Grace, you're going to scare her."

"Welcome to Angel's Orchard," Grace finished with a playful wink. "Feel free to explore up behind the estate. You'll find every variety of apples and plenty of peace."

"Thank you," Talie said softly, her smile mirroring Jesse's while he grabbed a few reusable bags. Together, they followed the winding path up into the orchard, embraced by the serenity of the rolling landscape.

"She is a close family friend. I've known her since I was a kid," he said. "She's got a heart of gold."

Talie nodded, a thoughtful expression settling across her features. "She seems special."

Jesse's steps slowed slightly, his gaze shifting toward her. "When I was fifteen, she had a heart attack. They declared her clinically dead, but she came back, against all odds. Ever since, she's had clairvoyant abilities."

"Has she ever predicted something that actually came true?"

"Yes, more times than I can count."

"That's incredible," she murmured, almost to herself.

His lips curved faintly, his tone carrying an easy warmth. "She could tell you stories all night long."

"I've always been fascinated by the paranormal. It intrigues me, but I'd be lying if I said it didn't scare me a little."

Jesse chuckled, his thumb brushing over her knuckles as he kept her hand firmly in his. "At first, I didn't like it when she'd warn me about people or tell me not to go to certain parties. But when everything she predicted started coming true… I had to take her seriously."

"She really does have a gift," she murmured, admiration brightening her voice.

Jesse paused, his gaze sweeping across the breathtaking landscape—the endless rows of trees, their branches heavy with apples, stretching out toward the mountains. "Yeah," he said, his voice low. "She does."

"Does she live here or in the country house?"

"In the country house," he replied, his eyes still fixed on the serene view. "The estate is for special events."

"It's truly beautiful."

"Every year during apple season, I come here. It's like heaven on earth."

"The Angel's Orchard," Talie murmured, her eyes taking in the lush green trees set against the vibrant blue sky. "The name fits perfectly."

"Take a look around," he said, leading her through the rows of apple trees.

Encouraging her with a small gesture, he led her deeper into the rows of apple trees. The path ahead stretched into a peaceful retreat, the air crisp and sweet with the scent of ripening fruit. The rustling of leaves formed a gentle symphony, grounding her in the present moment. Jesse's grip on her hand was steady and warm, a quiet reassurance as they strolled through the orchard.

Breaking the silence, Jesse glanced at her, his expression tinged with thoughtfulness. "You know, Grace told me about you."

Talie raised an eyebrow, curious. "About me?"

"She said I'd meet someone special this year," he began. "My soulmate, she called it. But she also said it wouldn't be easy, that I'd need a lot of patience to win her over."

Talie's heart skipped a beat, her gaze locking onto his deep blue eyes. "And what makes you think I'm that woman?" she asked, her voice barely above a whisper.

Jesse's lips curved into a slow, knowing smile. "Your resistance."

She drew a deep breath, the steadiness in her voice contrasting with the flicker of vulnerability in her eyes. "If I'm so resistant, it's because I'm looking for something serious."

Jesse took a bite of an apple, his eyes never leaving hers. Under his intense scrutiny, Talie felt a pang of guilt for not being completely honest. Her resistance wasn't only about wanting something serious—it was rooted in the deep-seated insecurities she carried about men and a lingering fear of betrayal.

You can trust him, she reminded herself, clinging to Grace's words like a lifeline. "Has Grace ever been wrong about her predictions?" she asked, her need for reassurance spilling into her tone.

"Never," he replied with quiet certainty, his gaze steady and unyielding.

As Jesse reached the last of the apples, Talie found her eyes drawn to him. When he stretched to pluck the highest fruit, the motion revealed two small dimples at the base of his back. She couldn't help but smile, her mind wandering to a conversation with Rebecca not long ago.

"What do you like most about Jesse physically? Rebecca had pressed with a playful grin.

"Well, his eyes are incredible, but I have to admit I'm obsessed with those little dimples on his lower back!"

Rebecca had burst into laughter. "Oh, the dimples of Apollo! There's something ridiculously sexy about those little indents."

"Dimples of Apollo? Talie had teased. "Quite the connoisseur, aren't we?"

"I read about them in high school when I was obsessed with anatomy. Trust me, they're sexy for a reason."

Jesse climbed down the ladder, catching Talie staring at him with a somewhat distracted look. "You okay?" he asked, his voice pulling her back to the present.

She blinked, her cheeks warming. "Yeah, I'm good."

Setting down his bag of apples, he reached for his ringing phone. "Yeah? I'm kind of busy," he said curtly. "I'll call you later." He ended the call, offering her an apologetic smile. "Let me show you another spot around here," he said, his hand extended toward her.

Just as she took it, his phone rang again. He sighed audibly this time, answering with visible irritation. "What's going on? Is it really important? I'm not in Montreal," he said, his tone a blend of annoyance and concern. "Okay, I get it. I'll try to be there within the next hour."

Hanging up, his expression had shifted, a heavier seriousness settling into his features. "I'm sorry."

"The club?" she asked, sensing the subtle shift in his mood.

Jesse nodded, his expression apologetic.

"I understand," she said, though disappointment surged through her. She quietly picked up her bag of apples and began walking down the path toward the country house.

Jesse hesitated, guilt washing over him. The perfect moment they'd been sharing now felt fractured. "Talie," he called after her, his voice softer. "I wonder if one day those doubts I see in you will disappear."

She stopped and turned to meet his gaze, her own emotions mirrored in the sincerity of his eyes.

"As long as I see those doubts," he continues, "I'll know I haven't fully convinced you yet."

Her voice was quiet but heavy with emotion. "Every moment with you convinces me more, but it's hard for me to accept that you won't fall for someone else at Club Viator."

His gaze was gentle, but unwavering. "Talie, it's because of the club that we're even here together today."

She glanced at the stunning mountains surrounding them, her mind drifting. *And it might be because of the club that we'll stop seeing each other one day…* The idea tied her stomach in knots, an ache she couldn't quite suppress.

They walked back to the Maserati, the weight of unspoken fears hanging between them. As they approached the car, Grace appeared, her warm eyes twinkling like sunlight through the orchard leaves. "Did you have fun?"

"Very much," Talie replied, managing a small smile. "The orchard is beautiful."

"You're welcome anytime, my dear," she said kindly before turning to Jesse, her gaze more serious, more probing. "Even though life is full of challenges, never doubt your inner strength, my boy."

Jesse nodded, sensing there was more to her words. "Thank you, Grace."

"Safe travels, kids," she said, kissing them both on the cheek. As they pulled away, the road kicked up a cloud of dust, the serene beauty of Angel's Orchard fading into the distance.

In the quiet of the drive, Jesse finally spoke. "If I hadn't been a dancer and we'd started dating seriously, would you have doubted my loyalty? Would you have worried I'd cheat on you?"

The question hit her like a wave, her throat tightening as her doubts and fears surfaced. Her gaze drifted to the scenic mountains, their beauty offering no distraction from the intensity of his words.

"Your fears aren't really about me being an exotic dancer, are they? They come from your past experiences," he continued.

"Probably," she admitted softly. The shadow of betrayal had kept her single for two years, a fear that would have followed her regardless of whether the man was a dancer, an executive, or an architect. It wasn't about Jesse's profession; it was about the scars she carried.

She cast her eyes downward, thinking of all the relationships she'd sabotaged in the name of self-preservation. "I guess I'll eventually conquer the demons of the past," she murmured, her words carrying more hope than certainty.

Jesse reached for her hand, giving it a reassuring squeeze. "Lucky for you, I'm a skilled fighter."

A slight smile tugged at her lips, the tension between them easing just enough. Yet her silence lingered, her fears still tightening around her chest. Speaking them aloud had lifted part of the burden, but true peace still felt distant, like the mountains stretching endlessly before them.

When they arrived at the agency, Jesse parked a few feet away. The silence from their drive clung to the moment, thick with tension, heavy with all the words left unsaid. Talie felt it pressing down on her, her thoughts swirling, trapping her in place.

Jesse waited, watching her, hoping she would turn toward him, but when she remained still, he gently reached over, tucking a stray strand of her hair behind her ear.

That simple, tender touch broke through her hesitation. She finally lifted her head, her eyes meeting his. The intensity in his gaze seemed to reach deep into her, pulling her closer to something she couldn't deny.

"Every moment I'm near you, this desire blazes inside me," he murmured, his voice rough with need. "I can't fight it anymore."

With agonizing slowness, he brushed his lips against hers, the brief contact sparking a wildfire of sensation. He paused, pulling back just enough to let the tension between them build, the air thick with anticipation. "I've been dreaming of this for so long," he whispered.

In one fluid motion, he closed the distance, capturing her lips in a deep, searing kiss. The world outside the car faded away, leaving only the fierce energy between their bodies. Jesse's kiss was raw, consuming, a force of nature that devoured her hesitation and left her reeling. Time seemed to stand still as they moved together, their lips and tongues entwined in a perfect blend of tenderness and hunger.

Talie melted into him, her body responding instinctively to his touch. His hands slid down her back, pulling her closer until there was no space left between them. Her fingers tangled in his hair, grounding her as waves of pleasure swept through her. The heat of his body, the taste of him on her lips—it was overwhelming, addictive. She felt herself unraveling in him, and she didn't want it to end.

When they finally pulled apart, their foreheads rested together while they caught their breath. Jesse's voice, low and husky, broke the silence. "Too bad I have to go," he murmured, the regret clear in his tone. His thumb traced the outline of her lips, swollen and sensitive from their kiss, leaving a trail of warmth in its wake.

Talie's heart fluttered, and without thinking, she ran the tip of her tongue over her lips, savoring the lingering taste of him. A playful smile tugged at her mouth while she adjusted her hair, her gaze locking onto his. "We'll finish this later," she whispered, reluctantly reaching for her bag of apples.

Just as she turned toward the door, Jesse caught her hand, spinning her back into his arms. His lips crashed onto hers with renewed urgency, making her drop the bag. Her arms wrapped around his neck, pulling him close like she couldn't bear to let go. The intensity of the kiss sent a rush of heat through her, leaving her breathless and weightless all at once.

When they finally parted, it was slow, their lips lingering as if neither wanted to break the connection.

"This… this is better than I ever imagined," she breathed, gazing into his sparkling blue eyes.

"You haven't seen anything yet," he murmured, his voice carrying a promise of more.

A smile curved her lips, and she leaned in, capturing him in one last, lingering kiss. "You've got to go," she whispered, her words tinged with reluctance while she slowly stepped back. She picked up her bag and slid out of the Maserati, the space between them making her heart ache with longing. As she walked away, the fire of their connection still burned within her, leaving her already yearning for the next time she'd be in his arms.

Seven

"So, how was it, girl?" Rebecca's voice crackled through the phone just as Talie answered.

Talie leaned against the counter, a soft smile tugging at her lips. "It was like a dream…"

"Where did he take you?"

"To the Angel's Orchard, in Saint-Joseph-du-Lac."

There was a pause. "Apple picking?" Rebecca sounded puzzled.

"Yes," she said, chuckling at her friend's disbelief.

"That's probably the last place I'd expect for a date."

"It was beautiful, Becca. A private orchard on this breathtaking estate."

"And Jesse?"

"You have no idea," she said, her words laced with a dreamy fondness that made Rebecca gasp.

"Did you two spend the night together?"

Talie's smile faltered slightly. "No… he got a call that cut our time short."

"A call?"

"The club," she admitted, her voice tinged with disappointment as she absently traced a finger along the edge of the counter.

Rebecca let out a soft sigh of understanding. "Ah. Are you upset?"

Talie hesitated, struggling to put her feelings into words. "Of course. I'm still wrapping my head around dating an exotic dancer… but I'm trying to remind myself that clothes don't make the man."

Rebecca snorted, breaking the tension with her usual humor. "Or the lack of them."

The scent of freshly squeezed orange juice filled Talie's kitchen, but her mind wasn't in the room. She kept replaying moments from the previous day—Jesse's lips on hers, the way his eyes smoldered every time he looked at her, as if she were the only woman in the world.

Her phone buzzed on the counter, interrupting her thoughts. Jesse's name lit up the screen, and her heart skipped a beat.

"Hello?" she said, her voice betraying the excitement she tried to hide.

"Morning," his deep voice greeted her.

"You're up early!" she said, glancing at the clock and raising an eyebrow.

"Didn't sleep much. Maybe four hours," he admitted, his tone light. "What's your plan for today?"

"Nothing yet."

"Beautiful day out. Want to do something?" His voice held a playful edge, and she could picture the grin tugging at his lips.

"What do you have in mind?"

"Do you have rollerblades?"

Talie let out a soft laugh. "I do, but it's been ages since I've used them."

"How about we skate along the Lachine Canal in Old Montreal?"

"Sounds perfect," she replied, the excitement bubbling in her chest.

"I'll pick you up in an hour?"

She glanced at the clock, already doing the mental math for how quickly she could get ready. "Perfect."

She hurried into the shower, her heart racing as the hot water cascaded over her skin, warming her inside and out. Her mind was already on the day ahead while she slipped into a pair of white shorts that hugged her sun-kissed legs, pairing them with a bikini top beneath a fitted pink and white tank. With her long hair tied in a loose ponytail, she added just a touch of makeup—enough to highlight her natural glow—then grabbed her rollerblades and essentials before rushing out the door.

As if on cue, Jesse's sleek Maserati pulled up in front of her apartment, the timing perfect. He stepped out, and her breath caught when his eyes swept over her in a slow, deliberate manner, darkening with appreciation.

"Hi," she managed, her voice catching slightly as she walked toward him, her steps charged with nervous energy.

"I'm glad we're picking up where we left off yesterday," he said, his gaze flicking to her lips, lingering there. "I couldn't stop thinking about them all night," he added, the words carrying a quiet intimacy, like a secret meant only for her.

Before she could respond, he leaned in, claiming her lips with a slow, sensual kiss. The tension melted away instantly, replaced by a surge of desire that made her feel weightless in his arms. As the kiss came to a natural pause, her heart was pounding, her breath uneven, and she could feel the electricity crackling between them. With a grin, Jesse reached for her rollerblades and held the car door open, his eyes never leaving hers.

She slid into the passenger seat, feeling like a teenager on her first crush all over again. Tucking one leg up to her chest, she idly traced her ankle with her fuchsia-painted nails, leaving faint white lines against her tanned skin. Jesse settled in beside her, his eyes lingering on the curve of her leg before traveling back up to meet hers. The way he looked at her sent a ripple of excitement through her. The air between them grew heavy, thick with the intoxicating pull of desire and anticipation.

Jesse exhaled sharply, his voice low and edged with hunger. "You have no idea how damn hard it is to focus on the road when you look like that."

A soft laugh escaped her, her cheeks warming under his intense stare. The hum of the engine filled the space as they finally pulled away. Jesse turned up the radio, and the unmistakable opening notes of Depeche Mode's 'Strangelove' filled the car.

"I love this band!" she exclaimed, her face lighting up with excitement.

"Me too," he said, matching her energy and turning the volume up. He glanced at her, eyes crinkling with amusement while they both joined in, singing loudly, their voices intertwining with the melody.

"Strangelove. Strange highs and strange lows. Strangelove. That's how my love goes. Strangelove. Will you give it to me?"

As the song faded out, Jesse stopped at a red light, his hand sliding up her bare thigh, fingers tracing a lazy, teasing path along her skin. His voice dropped to a husky whisper, and with a crooked smirk, he murmured the final lyric to her, each word wrapped in heat and challenge. "Will you give it to me?"

The streets of Old Montreal buzzed with life, laughter and conversation mingling with the rhythmic clatter of their skates against cobblestones. The sun drenched everything in a golden warmth, and Talie felt the city's infectious energy seep into her. She glanced at Jesse, who skated beside her, his relaxed confidence adding to the charm of the moment.

"Every time I come here, it feels like a mini vacation," she said, weaving around a pedestrian.

They glided onto the bike path, the city gradually giving way to scenic greenery. For a while, they skated in companionable silence, the wind teasing her hair. Eventually, they stopped by a shaded bench to catch their breath and sip water.

Jesse leaned back, his gaze drifting over the path ahead. "If you're up for it, we could check out the Atwater Market. Grab some lunch, maybe?" he suggested, his tone light and inviting as he pulled off his shirt. "There are a few great spots nearby where we can eat."

Talie's eyes followed his movements, her fingers itching to run over his skin. His torso was a work of art—arms, shoulders, and abs sculpted with precision, exuding a natural, effortless sexiness that stood out from the overworked physiques of fitness magazines or the flashy aesthetics of club dancers.

When he caught her staring, a smirk tugged at the corner of his mouth. "You've never looked at me like that at Club Viator."

She met his gaze, unashamed, a small smile playing on her lips. "It's different now," she admitted, her eyes roving over him. "I don't see you the same way anymore."

Jesse stepped closer, reaching for her hands. His touch was warm, grounding. He brought her hands to his neck, pulling her gently into him until their bodies touched. His lips brushed hers, tentative and teasing, before deepening into a kiss that left her breathless. She felt herself melt into him, her fingers curling against his skin as their shared heat grew, feeding the intensity of the moment.

"Talie," he whispered against his lips, his hands tightening around her waist.

She smiled, leaning back slightly, her breath still catching in her chest. His gaze dipped to the enticing curve of her neckline, lingering. "What was that about lunch again?" she teased.

He chuckled, the sound deep and rich, like velvet. "Come on," he said, grabbing his shirt and their water bottles.

The Atwater Market bustled with life, the scent of fresh produce and baked goods mingling in the air. They picked out a few items, and Jesse led them to a quiet park nearby, where they settled beneath a shady tree. Talie popped a cherry tomato into her mouth, savoring its burst of flavor.

"I've never met a guy who's this committed to eating clean," she said, watching him unwrap a fresh salad. "Most people think this lifestyle is restrictive, but they don't get how artificial food messes with everything."

He nodded, his expression thoughtful. "They're disconnected," he said simply. "They don't realize how much it affects their energy, their mood, their health."

Talie watched him closely, captivated by the depth of his understanding. How could someone so in tune with himself have avoided serious relationships for so long?

"You seem deep in thought," he remarked, catching the distant look in her eyes.

She hesitated, but her curiosity got the better of her. "I just don't get why you never wanted a serious relationship before," she said, her voice soft but direct. "You're caring, sensitive, passionate." Her gaze searched his, her voice lowering. "The more I get to know you, the less I believe it."

Jesse's silence spoke volumes, shadows passing through his eyes. He looked away, taking a slow sip of water as if weighing his response. "I didn't want to tie myself down," he finally said, his voice quiet, tinged with a sadness that caught her off guard.

She leaned closer, trying to catch his gaze. For a moment, she thought he might open up, but instead, he glanced at the ground, his expression unreadable. The air between them grew heavier, the unspoken words hanging like a veil of uncertainty.

As Jesse knelt to adjust his rollerblades, she watched him closely, hoping for a sign—anything that might offer a glimpse beneath his guarded exterior. But when he straightened and looked at her, his face gave nothing away. Whatever emotions churned beneath the surface, he kept them well-guarded, the invisible walls around him holding firm.

They skated back onto the path, the midday sun beating down relentlessly. Talie slowed her pace, her skin glistening with sweat. Without a second thought, she tugged off her tank top, leaving only her bikini top beneath. The breeze kissed her bare shoulders, offering much-needed relief.

Jesse's eyes flicked to her, tracking the graceful curve of her waist and stomach, following her movements. His expression softened, as if the tension he carried melted away in her presence. For a moment, it felt like time paused, leaving only the quiet admiration of a man captivated by her unfiltered beauty.

A group of girls skated past, their wide-eyed stares unmistakably directed at Jesse, tracing every line and detail of his body. He gave them a casual nod, but the girls' excitement was barely contained, their heads turning back for a second glance.

"You just made their day," Talie said, a smirk playing on her lips.

Jesse ran a hand through his hair, his grin as dazzling as the sunlight. "You think so?"

"Absolutely," she replied, fully aware of the magnetic pull he had on others.

The path led them through a picturesque landscape, with trees casting intermittent shade, offering a welcome reprieve from the sun. The birds chirped in the branches above, and the scent of wildflowers filled the air, adding to the peacefulness of the moment.

When they reached Old Montreal, the cobblestone streets guided them to a quaint little ice cream shop by the river. They settled into a bench with a perfect view of the calm, rippling water. Jesse grew quiet, his gaze fixed on the river, his thoughts seemingly miles away.

"You must be getting tired," Talie ventured, trying to understand his sudden silence. "I would've given up long ago if I'd only slept for three or four hours."

Jesse's hand drifted to her thigh, his touch warm and grounding. "The body adapts to the rhythm you set for it," he said, a faint smile tugging at the corners of his mouth. "I still have plenty of energy to spare."

"Are you working tonight?"

"No." His eyes locked onto hers with that same seductive intensity she had come to know so well. "You have plans?"

She hesitated, her heartbeat quickening under his steady attention. "Uh… no."

"Good," he murmured, his fingers tracing absentminded patterns against her skin.

"I guess it's tough for you to go to bed early when you're not working," she said, steering the conversation elsewhere.

Jesse's smirk returned, playful and unguarded. "I never fall asleep before midnight."

"For me, midnight is the exception."

"Then the nights you come to the club are exceptional nights, right?" he teased.

Talie smiled at him but quickly turned her gaze to the river, realizing she no longer wanted to step foot in the club now that Jesse was becoming more than just a fleeting presence in her life. "…were exceptional nights," she corrected quietly.

Jesse's brow furrowed as he studied her. Intrigued, he leaned in, trying to grasp the deeper meaning behind her words.

"I don't think I can go back there, Jesse. My feelings for you have changed," she said softly, her confession trembling on her lips.

He nodded slowly, sensing her inner turmoil. "I understand."

As she tried to process her own words, Jesse broke the silence, his tone softer than before. "When I started working at the club, I wasn't single," he began, his eyes still fixed on hers.

Talie felt a pang in her chest, sensing that something important was about to be revealed.

He exhaled deeply, the weight of his confession settling in the tight set of his shoulders. "I was with a woman for over a year. She wasn't thrilled about my new job, but she liked the money," he began, his voice subdued, each word measured. "With her expensive tastes, she saw it as a chance to turn many of her dreams into reality."

He paused, running a hand through his hair. The vulnerability in his movements was disarming, revealing a side of him Talie hadn't seen before. "She came to the club regularly," he continued, his gaze distant, reliving the memories. "She'd sit in the back, watching my private dances. Then, she'd go home… devastated. It was slowly killing her."

His voice softened to a whisper, and Talie's chest tightened. She could see the echoes of her own fears mirrored in his story.

"Our relationship unraveled, and… I started cheating on her," he admitted, holding her gaze as she struggled to catch her breath.

The raw honesty in his voice cut through her, each word landing like a heavy blow. The gravity of his words hung between them, a tangible reminder of the complexities of love and trust.

"I know this is what you fear most about us," he continued, his eyes searching hers for understanding. "I saw it in your eyes the first time we connected. That's why I waited to tell you—because I knew that one wrong move, and you'd walk away."

Talie's gaze dropped to the river, her thoughts swirling like the current before them. Emotions churned within her, uncertain and relentless.

Jesse reached out, his voice steady but filled with quiet resolve. "I've told you before, and I'll keep telling you if I have to. You're not just a fling to me. I wouldn't have waited this long for something shallow. I'm done with that life."

She looked up, searching his face, trying to find the truth in his words. "Did you tell her?" she asked, her voice trembling with unspoken emotion.

He hesitated, his voice barely above a whisper. "She killed herself."

His words hung heavily in the air, his revelation pressing down on them like an unseen force. Talie's hand flew to her mouth as a sob caught in her throat, her eyes welling with tears. She reached for him instinctively, wrapping her arms around his neck and pulling him close. Her face pressed against the warmth of his skin, tears soaking his shirt. He held her tightly, his arms encircling her in a desperate attempt to keep the pain at bay. They stayed like that for what felt like an eternity, cocooned in shared sorrow and silent understanding.

What a terrible price to pay for his mistakes, she thought, her heart aching for him. No one deserved to carry guilt like this forever.

"You have to trust me," he whispered, his voice cracking under the strain of his emotions. "I've spent years trying to cope with this. But now…I'm finally ready to move on."

She wanted to believe him—needed to. Searching his eyes for any lingering doubt, all she found was a man stripped of pretense, baring his soul, silently asking for her trust. She nodded faintly, allowing the moment to settle between them, letting the silence offer its quiet solace.

With heavy hearts, they resumed their walk, hand in hand. Jesse broke the stillness with a quiet determination. "For years, I thought I needed to be alone… or at least that's what I told myself. But now, I see it differently. I just hadn't met someone like you."

Talie's heart pounded, her voice a fragile breath as she dared to ask, "And what if you're wrong again?"

Jesse paused mid-step, turning to face her fully. "You don't make that kind of mistake twice."

Then, with infinite tenderness, he leaned in and kissed her, sealing his vow with a touch that conveyed everything words could not.

Eight

Leaning against the kitchen island, Jesse's gaze followed Talie, mesmerized by the sway of her curves as she moved, preparing a light meal.

"Sure you don't want a little help?" he asked for the second time, his voice playful yet edged with genuine insistence.

Talie turned to him, the hint of a smile tugging at her lips. She retrieved a bottle of wine and set it before him with a teasing glint in her eye. "Well, if you're that eager to assist, how about you pour us a glass?" Her tone was light, but her gaze lingered on him, charming and coy.

Jesse's grin widened, reaching for the bottle. "Now that," he said, uncorking it with ease, "I can handle." He poured generously into two glasses and set hers beside her on the counter. But as she reached for it, he leaned in close, his lips grazing the curve of her neck. The faint scent of her perfume wrapped around him, making it impossible to step away.

He stayed close, stealing soft kisses and teasing nibbles whenever she wasn't looking, his presence a constant, magnetic pull. The kitchen, once a simple space, became their private haven, humming with the electric chemistry between them.

When they finally sat down to eat, the lighthearted mood began to shift, their conversation dipping into deeper waters. Talie cautiously ventured into the shadowed chapter of his life after his ex's tragic death. He recounted the torment he had endured—endless days steeped in darkness and the long therapy sessions that had gradually helped him piece himself back together.

"Didn't Club Viator's bosses say anything when they found you completely wasted? she asked, concern softening her voice.

Jesse's expression darkened slightly. "It was pretty tame compared to all the illegal stuff going on there."

Her eyebrows arched in intrigue. "Illegal stuff?"

He hesitated for a moment before adding, "The place is run by Italians, Talie," he said, his tone heavy with implication.

He looked away momentarily, then back at her, holding her gaze for a long, intense beat. He could see the curiosity flickering in her eyes. She clearly wasn't going to settle for such a vague answer.

"Come on," she urged, leaning closer. "You can't just leave me hanging like that."

He chuckled but shook his head firmly. "I know you can handle it, but there's no point in dragging you into that world."

"Jesse," she purred, giving him a seductive look, hoping to coax more information from him. With a smooth motion, she swept her hair over one shoulder, drawing his attention to her neckline.

He smirked at her attempt to pry the truth out of him. "You're playing a dangerous game. Don't tempt me."

"And what exactly am I risking?" she teased, leaning in until their breaths mingled.

Jesse's gaze flicked to her lips, his restraint hanging by a thread. "That I might stop holding back," he said, his eyes darkening with desire.

"Is that supposed to scare me?" she whispered.

In one swift movement, his hands gripped her waist, lifting her onto the kitchen table. His gaze swept over her, lingering on her cleavage before drifting lower, tracing every curve with an intensity that stripped her bare without a single touch. Leaning in, his lips brushed her ear as he murmured, "You're risking a lot more than you think."

Their eyes met, and in that instant, an unspoken understanding flared to life, igniting something primal between them. Without breaking eye contact, Jesse stripped off his shirt, revealing the sculpted lines of his torso. She'd seen every inch of him before, yet the sight still stole her breath. Instinctively, her fingers reached out, tracing the firm ridges of his chest and abs, lingering as if memorizing him all over again. Beneath her touch, his muscles tensed, and a low, guttural groan rumbled from his throat.

Before she could take another breath, his lips crushed hers in a kiss that was as fierce as it was unrelenting. His hands moved with purpose, stripping her top away in a single, effortless pull. His gaze devoured her, drinking her in before his touch followed, hot and possessive. The curve of her breast, the taut line of her stomach—each caress sent waves of anticipation rolling through her.

"I have condoms in my room," she murmured, her voice a trembling whisper.

Jesse didn't reply. Instead, he swept her into his arms, carrying her to the sanctuary of her bedroom, a place untouched by any man since her last heartbreak. He eased her onto the bed, and just as she reached for the condoms in her nightstand, his fingers wrapped around her wrist. "Not so fast," he murmured, his voice thick with intent.

His hands roamed over her, worshipping her with reverence. He slid her shorts down, his movements measured, making her breath hitch. His fingers teased the edge of her thong, tracing the delicate fabric with an agonizing slowness that made her tremble beneath him. She felt exposed yet powerful, captivated by the hunger in his gaze.

"I want you so much," he confessed, his voice hoarse with desire.

His eyes, dark and ravenous, roamed over her, savoring every curve, imprinting the image in his memory. He leaned in, lips grazing her collarbone, trailing downward in slow, reverent kisses that set her skin ablaze.

Every touch was unhurried, every movement restrained, pulsating with need.

"Jesse," she breathed, his name a plea and a promise all at once.

His hands moved to his jeans, slipping them off with the same controlled ease that had stripped away her defenses. Slowly, teasingly, he pushed down his boxer briefs, revealing the undeniable evidence of his arousal. The sharp rip of the condom wrapper sliced through the thick silence, punctuating the moment as he rolled it on with practiced confidence.

Positioning himself between her thighs, he hovered, his weight balanced above her, gaze locked onto hers. The intensity in his eyes stole her breath, grounding her in the present, in him. Slowly, he eased into her, and the sensation shattered her, a gasp slipping past her lips while her body molded to his. His own groan vibrated through the space between them, coiling around her like an invisible tether. The world faded away. There was only this. Only them. She arched into him, her fingers digging into the firm muscles of his back, nails leaving fiery trails in their wake.

"Look at me," he murmured, his voice a breath against her lips.

Her eyes fluttered open, meeting his, and the raw desire blazing in his gaze stole the last breath from her lungs. There was no denying the depth of the moment—the way it transcended the physical, reaching into something more profound, something neither of them could name.

"I want you to remember this," he whispered, his breath hot against her skin. "Every second."

His lips found her throat, igniting a trail of heat with every kiss, while his hands claimed her curves, savoring the way her body responded to him. He moved with aching slowness, each roll of his hips pulling her deeper into the storm of him.

Time seemed to blur as her body surrendered to his completely, every nerve alive under his touch. She lifted her hips to meet him, her hands clutching his arms desperately, seeking an anchor while the tension within her spiraled higher, ready to shatter.

"Jesse," she gasped, her voice breaking on his name. It spurred him on, his movements growing more demanding, more consuming, a blinding crescendo that wiped away every thought, every breath.

The moment stretched impossibly until a soft, breathless cry escaped her lips, his groan following close behind as they tumbled into release together. Their movements stilled, the world slowly returning, but the intimacy lingered like an invisible bond tethering them to each other.

Jesse's fingers laced through hers, pinning her hands above her head, his gaze softening. "You've only had a glimpse of what's to come."

With one last lingering kiss, he slipped away to the bathroom, leaving her sprawled across the bed, heart pounding, mind spinning.

As her breathing steadied, her gaze wandered to his back, noticing the red streaks her nails had left on his skin. It had been over two years since she'd been with anyone, but nothing in her memory came close to this.

Jesse returned to the bed, his eyes roaming over her naked body like an artist admiring his finest masterpiece. Sitting on the edge of the mattress, he let his fingers glide over her skin, tracing a slow path along her side.

"I've never felt so desired by a man," she whispered softly.

His lips curved into a faint smile, and he wrapped an arm around her waist, pulling her close until their bodies were flush again. His kiss, deep and unrelenting, left her breathless all over again, her fingers tangling in his hair as the moment threatened to consume her.

"Are we well stocked?" he asked, tilting his head toward the nightstand.

Talie jolted awake to the blaring alarm clock, her body still humming with echoes of the night before. Condom wrappers lay scattered across the floor, quiet reminders of their unrestrained passion. Her gaze shifted to Jesse, sprawled peacefully on his stomach, his back marked by long, red scratches that trailed down to the curve of his butt—evidence of the pleasure he'd given her. Warmth bloomed through her at the memory, her lips curving into a private, satisfied smile. Slipping out of bed quietly, she headed to the shower, the water invigorating her skin and washing away the last traces of sleep.

"Hey, girl!" Rebecca called out as Talie walked into the office.

"Hey," she replied, her glow impossible to miss.

"Oh my gosh! That face—you had one hell of a night!" Rebecca exclaimed, pulling her into a playful hug.

Talie laughed and gently pushed her away, making her way to her desk. "A *lot* of pleasure," she added, her voice dreamy and light, unable to hide the satisfaction from her friend.

"It's been ages since I've seen you this lit up! Looks like your Jesse took you straight to cloud nine."

"And I haven't come down yet," she said, the memory of the night still fresh in her mind.

"Sex is a drug, girl."

"Well, I just found my new addiction."

Jesse woke up in Talie's bed, feeling the blissful exhaustion from their night together. Wandering into the kitchen, he spotted the note she'd left: *See you tonight.* Beside it lay a key to her front door. A satisfied smile tugged at his lips while he poured himself a glass of water, the memories of her body, her laughter, and the fire they had shared washing over him. But just as he let himself revel in it, his phone buzzed. Seeing Clayton's name flash on the screen, Jesse's relaxed expression hardened. He answered, listening intently, his frown deepening with each passing second.

As the workday came to an end, Talie stepped out of the office with a radiant smile. Her friends had spent the day peppering her with questions, but she had artfully dodged them, keeping the intimate details of her night with Jesse to herself. It still felt surreal—they had made love nearly the entire night. The memory sent a flutter of heat through her, quickening her steps with growing anticipation. She couldn't wait to relive the magic.

By the time she got home, something felt off. Jesse's car wasn't in the parking lot. Her smile faltered when she unlocked the door, half-expecting to find him waiting inside. But the apartment greeted her with silence. A folded note on the counter immediately caught her attention. *I have to leave for a few days. Something's going down at the club. I'll try to call you, but don't reach out to me. Not on my phone, not at the club. Don't worry, gorgeous.*

Her breath caught as she read the note over and over again, her heart racing. What was happening? Was he in danger? She clutched the note, her mind spinning with worst-case scenarios.

Stumbling to her bedroom, she collapsed onto the bed, tears spilling down her cheeks. All day, she had looked forward to seeing him again, to reliving the pleasure they had shared. But now, something dark and unsettling had entered her world, casting a shadow over the happiness she had found with him. It felt like her heart was being ripped apart. She hugged her pillow, clinging to the faint traces of his scent, trying to find comfort, but the fear gnawed at her, leaving her helpless.

The night stretched on endlessly. Questions and doubts circled her mind, refusing to let her rest. Was he safe? Why couldn't she contact him? By 2 AM, the realization hit: there would be no call tonight. Exhausted and emotionally drained, she finally drifted into a fitful sleep, praying that he was safe, wherever he was.

The next morning at the agency, Rebecca was quick to pull her into a hug. "Have you heard from him?" she asked, her voice filled with concern.

Talie shook her head, her worry etched clearly on her face. "No, not yet."

Rebecca frowned. "Are you worried?"

"Terribly," she admitted. "I'm afraid he's in danger."

"Did he ever tell you anything about the club?"

Talie hesitated. "Not really… just that it's run by Italians."

Rebecca's eyes widened. "The mafia?"

"I guess so," she murmured, the reality sinking in.

Her friend placed a reassuring hand on her arm. "Spiraling into worst-case scenarios won't help."

"I know," she replied, her voice shaky. "But it's so hard just sitting here, waiting for him to call."

Rebecca didn't say anything, simply pulling her into another hug, this one tighter and more protective. The smile Talie offered in return was fragile, and as Rebecca held her, the dam finally broke. Tears spilled freely, every sob releasing the fear and tension that had been tightening inside her since the moment she found Jesse's note.

The days that followed were an emotional whirlwind for Talie, leaving her teetering on the edge of madness. Every second was spent anxiously waiting for Jesse to reach out. Nights were sleepless, her thoughts a torrent of terrifying possibilities. At the agency, her focus crumbled, her energy drained by worry.

"Your phone rang," Claudia said, watching Talie step out of the bathroom, eyes puffy and red, her expression hollow.

Talie froze. Hope surged as she rushed to her desk, snatching up her phone. Her breath caught while she listened to the voicemail, her hands trembling slightly.

"Talie, meet me at one o'clock at Square St. Louis. I'll wait for fifteen minutes. If you can't come, I'll reach out later. Don't try to call me. I'm okay, don't worry."

The relief came in waves, crashing into her all at once. "It was him," she whispered, turning to Claudia with wide, teary eyes. "He wants me to meet him at Square St. Louis at one o'clock." She glanced at the clock on the wall—time was running out.

"Go! Hurry!" Claudia urged.

Talie didn't need to be told twice. She grabbed her things and bolted out the door, her heart pounding with both hope and fear. Behind the wheel of her car, her thoughts spun faster than the engine. Her hands tightened on the steering wheel, pushing forward, barely noticing the traffic around her.

The parking gods were kind—she found a spot close to Square St. Louis and hurried down the street, almost breaking into a sprint. When she spotted Jesse sitting on a bench, a cap pulled low over his eyes, her heart slammed against her ribs. Relief mixed with a wave of emotion so intense she could barely breathe.

Jesse stood as soon as he spotted her, closing the distance in seconds. Talie barely registered his arms wrapping around her before the tears came, spilling out in raw sobs. She clung to him, burying her face in his shoulder while he murmured soft reassurances, his hands gentle on her back.

"Don't cry," he whispered.

She looked up at him, eyes still swimming with unshed tears. "I was so worried."

He leaned in and kissed her, a kiss that spoke of all the emotions he couldn't put into words, his lips lingering on hers, trying to erase the distance of the past few days.

When he pulled back, his hand found hers, fingers intertwining as he led her to sit beside him on the bench. For a moment, silence hung between them, weighted and fragile. Jesse broke it first.

"Diego, the owner of Club Viator, was arrested," he began, his tone low and steady.

Talie's stomach twisted. "Arrested?"

"The police are interrogating everyone who worked closely with him. They're digging deep, looking for anything they can use."

"Have you… talked to them?" she asked, fear creeping into her words.

His eyes flicked away, avoiding hers. "I can't."

Her breath hitched, and she couldn't stop the tremor in her voice. "Jesse, you're not… involved in anything illegal, are you?"

He ran a hand through his hair, and when he finally turned back, his eyes were clouded, haunted. "Let's just say, after all this time working there, I've seen things.

Heard things. Enough to make me a problem for some very dangerous people."

Talie's fingers began to drum nervously on her thighs, her face growing paler by the second. Jesse could sense the fear radiating from her, and guilt surged through him for pulling her into this mess.

"Certain people connected to Diego have made it clear that I need to disappear. They're giving me an out. If I keep quiet and vanish, the police won't find me," he said, his voice laden with tension.

Talie's heart dropped. "Vanish? Jesse, what are you saying?"

"A new identity. A clean break," he said, his voice quieter now, as if saying it out loud made it more real.

"What?" she gasped.

He reached for her hands, holding them firmly, anchoring her to him. "Talie, this is the only way I can keep you safe. If I stay… I'm putting both of us in danger."

"So you just run? Leave everything behind? Leave me behind?"

"It's not forever," he said, his voice low but resolute. "Just until things cool down."

Talie's gaze drifted past him, her thoughts spinning, trying to grasp the enormity of what he was saying. The words settled heavily, suffocating her resolve.

"You can't tell anyone," he continued, his tone soft yet firm. "If people ask, just say I'm going abroad for a while."

Her eyes snapped back to his, shimmering with unshed tears. "I'll help you, Jesse," she murmured. "But I don't want to live a life full of lies. I don't want to hide."

"I know," he whispered, his voice breaking as he pulled her into his arms. She buried her face in his neck, breathing him in, wishing she could freeze the moment, hold onto him forever.

"This is unbearable," she choked out, her heart twisting in pain.

Jesse cupped her face, his fingers gently brushing away the tears that streaked her cheeks. "I'll get in touch the moment everything is settled," he promised. "I just need to make sure everything is safe before we see each other again."

He kissed her gently, lingering to memorize the feel of her lips, fearing it might be the last time. "Please, be careful," she whispered, her voice trembling.

"I will," he promised, holding her gaze for one last, endless moment, before turning and disappearing into the crowd.

Talie stood motionless, her heart caught in the tug-of-war between fear and hope. Jesse's words pressed heavily on her chest, making it hard to breathe. She finally forced herself to move, dragging her feet back to the car. As she sat behind the wheel and merged onto the road, the chaos in her mind refused to settle, spinning in frantic, endless loops. Jesse's revelation consumed her thoughts, blurring the world beyond the windshield. The sudden halt of the car in front of her snapped her back to reality. Her heart leaped as she yanked the wheel to the side, narrowly avoiding a collision. The screech of tires rang in her ears, her pulse hammering, adrenaline surging through her veins.

"Damn it," she muttered, shaking her head. She turned up the radio, desperate to drown out the turmoil in her mind.

By the time she arrived at the agency, her friends were waiting, their eyes full of questions.

"Well?" they asked the moment she walked through the door.

Talie hesitated, her gaze dropping to the floor. "There's something serious going on at the club," she said quietly, her words measured and careful.

"And Jesse?" Claudia pressed.

Talie swallowed hard, keeping her eyes fixed on her hands as they twisted nervously in her lap. "He's… going abroad for a while," she mumbled. "Just until things settle down."

Rebecca immediately enveloped her in a warm hug. "Oh, my girl," she murmured.

Laurence's concern deepened. "Do you know where he's going?"

Talie shook her head, her voice barely above a whisper. "He can't tell me."

A heavy silence fell over them. She hated keeping secrets, especially from the people who cared about her most, but Jesse's safety demanded her silence.

Despite their support, an icy loneliness wrapped around her heart. She wasn't ready to lose Jesse, but the thought of living a life filled with uncertainty, fear, and half-truths terrified her even more.

"Hey, girl!" Rebecca's voice burst through the office like a breath of fresh air, her infectious energy lighting up the room.

"Hey," Talie mumbled, not bothering to lift her eyes from the computer screen in front of her. The weight of the past week hung heavily on her shoulders, dulling her usual spark.

Rebecca slid into the chair beside her. "So, I've got this soirée planned at my place tonight—some food, and way too much wine. You're coming. No excuses."

Talie's lips twitched, the faintest hint of a smile breaking through. Rebecca's persistence was hard to resist. She hadn't realized how much she needed this—a distraction, a lifeline to something normal. For days, she'd been drowning in her thoughts, struggling to maintain her composure. But now, as Rebecca's warmth nudged at her defenses, she felt the cracks beginning to form.

"Okay, but if I come, no talking about Jesse. Promise me," she said, her voice quiet but firm.

Rebecca grinned, crossing her heart with a flourish. "Promise. We'll keep it light—just good vibes and zero drama."

Talie nodded, grateful for her friend's understanding. "Alright. Who's coming?"

"Just the girls from the agency, David, and maybe one or two of his friends."

Talie raised a skeptical brow. "No setups, right?"

Rebecca's eyes sparkled with mischief, but she held her hands up in mock innocence. "Would I ever?"

Later that evening, the warm spray of the shower beat against Talie's skin, washing away the tension that had clung to her all day. Steam fogged the glass, and as she stepped out, she caught a glimpse of her reflection in the mirror. Her face looked thinner, her features more drawn than she remembered. The stress of the last week was etched plainly across her expression. She sighed, reaching for a towel to dry off, but froze mid-step.

Jesse stood there, leaning casually against the vanity, his bare chest framed by his strong, sculpted arms. His once-familiar hair, now dyed black as night, fell in tousled waves around his face, making him look even more dangerously untamed. The piercing brilliance of his eyes contrasted sharply with the dark mess of his hair, locking her in place. A thin, black tattoo curled around his bicep and trailed down to his side, its fresh ink adding a seductive edge to his presence.

"Miss me?" His voice was low and gravelly, teasing, with an undertone of something deeper.

She moved to grab the towel, but Jesse was quicker—too quick. With a swift, fluid motion, he plucked it from her grasp, leaving her exposed under his intense gaze.

"Jesse…" she started, but her words faltered under the weight of his presence.

He stepped forward, closing the space between them until nothing remained. The warmth of his body overwhelmed her, and she gasped softly when her back met the cool tiles of the wall. Before she could process what was happening, Jesse lifted her effortlessly, her legs instinctively wrapping around his waist. His lips claimed hers in an instant, the kiss consuming, reclaiming every second they'd lost.

"I've missed you," he murmured against her mouth, his hands roaming her body with a need that bordered on desperation.

"Me too," she whispered, voice trembling, fingers tangled in his hair, pulling him closer. A nervous laugh escaped her, unbidden yet tender, as she admitted, "When I was younger, I used to fantasize about bad boys with tattoos."

He pulled back just enough to smirk at her. "And do I live up to the fantasy?"

"You've far surpassed it," she confessed, her fingers tracing the dark lines of his new tattoo.

As the intensity of their passion softened into something deeper, Talie studied his face, noting the subtle changes—the weariness in his eyes, the tension etched into his features. "This past week has been torture," she whispered, her voice heavy with emotion. "I couldn't stop thinking about you."

Jesse cupped her face, his thumb brushing away a stray droplet of water. "It's been hard for me too."

Her heart ached at the raw vulnerability in his eyes. She reached up, cradling his face in her hands, wanting to soothe the pain she saw there. Just as their lips met in a deep, soul-searching kiss, her phone chimed from the counter, breaking the moment. "Oh no! I forgot about Rebecca!" Her eyes widened with a mixture of guilt and panic.

Jesse stepped back slightly, an amused smile tugging at his lips. "Got plans tonight?"

"I was supposed to have dinner with Becca, but..." She hesitated, her desire to stay with him tugging fiercely at her resolve. "I'll cancel. I want to stay with you."

His hands slid down her arms, their warmth grounding her. "Go to your dinner."

"But Jesse, we need to talk. I've been drowning this week, hiding in my office, barely holding it together." Her voice quavered as she searched his eyes for reassurance.

"We'll talk tomorrow morning. I promise," he said, his hands trailing slow, teasing paths over her skin. "I've got a few things to take care of tonight. Go, enjoy yourself."

"Are you staying here tonight?" she asked, her heart fluttering with hope.

Jesse's expression darkened with a playful yet undeniable promise. "Staying? I'm planning on doing much more than just staying," he said, his voice rich with intent. He leaned in close, his lips brushing the shell of her ear. "By the time I'm done, you won't remember anything else."

The door swung open with Rebecca's characteristic enthusiasm, her smile wide and contagious. "My girl! We've been waiting for you!"

"I'm so sorry, Becca," Talie said, stepping inside as a rush of noise and energy enveloped her. The living room was alive, buzzing with laughter, chatter, and the steady rhythm of upbeat music.

She wove through the crowd, her gaze landing on two men lounging on the plush sofa, their postures relaxed yet attentive the moment they noticed her approach.

"You remember David, don't you?" Rebecca asked with a knowing twinkle in her eye.

Talie nodded, offering a polite smile. "Of course."

David's confident grin widened, his eyes lingering on her a fraction too long.

"And this is Josh, his friend," Rebecca continued, motioning toward the quieter man seated next to David.

"Hi," Talie greeted, her tone polite but distant. Josh's eyes met hers, and she quickly averted her gaze, the intensity of his stare making her skin prickle.

Before the moment could stretch too long, Claudia and Laurence stumbled out of the kitchen, their arms draped around each other as they dissolved into giggles.

"Where have you been?" Claudia teased, her voice lilting with tipsiness. "Got lost on the way here?"

Talie managed a small laugh, shaking her head. "No, just exhausted. Took a quick nap and almost overslept."

"Well, you're here now," Rebecca interjected, slipping an arm around her shoulders. "Come on, let me get you a drink."

"I'll have whatever you're having," she said, exchanging polite smiles with a few other guests before settling into the cozy living room. She tried to relax, to let the rhythm of the party distract her, but Josh's eyes were on her again, his gaze unwavering and too bold for her comfort.

"So, what have you been up to lately?" David asked, smoothly steering the conversation.

"I'm still working at the agency with Rebecca. What about you?"

"Busy," David said, launching into a story about his latest construction projects. "Josh joined the team a few months ago."

"Really?" she replied, glancing at Josh briefly.

"Yeah, it's been good," he added, his eyes still fixed on her.

She nodded as Rebecca reappeared with drinks in hand, her presence easing some of the tension. But the longer the evening stretched, Talie's discomfort only grew. David's boasting grated on her nerves, and Josh's attention felt suffocating. Even Claudia and Laurence, usually a source of lighthearted fun, were lost in their own tipsy bubble.

By the time Rebecca announced dinner, Talie was ready to leave. She joined the others at the table, picking at her food as conversations blurred into background noise. Rebecca perched on David's lap, giggling and playfully nibbling his ear, while Josh sat nearby, his gaze still straying to Talie. Her detachment grew, and before dessert was even served, she stood up.

"Oh, come on, you're not leaving already!" Claudia protested, her voice loud and slurred.

She offered a faint smile, stifling a yawn. "Yes. I'm really exhausted. See you on Monday?"

"Oh, right! You've got the weekend off!" Rebecca hugged her tightly. "Thanks for coming. Did you have fun?"

"I was a bit tired," she said, "but we'll do it again sometime…"

After bidding quick farewells to the other guests, she left, a sense of relief washing over her. Back at her apartment, she sank into her couch and picked up a book, hoping it would help clear her mind. Two chapters in, her eyelids grew heavy, and sleep gently overtook her—until a soft whisper pulled her from the depths of slumber. Jesse's voice, low and familiar, drifted through the living room. "Hey," he murmured, settling down beside her.

Talie blinked sleepily, propping herself up on one elbow to face him. "Hey," she replied, her voice still thick with sleep.

"Did you have a good evening?"

She sighed, rubbing her eyes. "Awful," she admitted with a wry smile.

"Awful?" he echoed, tucking a stray strand of her long hair behind her ear.

"The girls were really drunk, and I was stuck with two guys who bored me to death," she said, a laugh bubbling up despite herself. "I even considered making a daring escape through the window."

His chuckle was low, rich, a sound that settled warmly in her chest. "Sounds like quite the evening," Jesse teased, the corners of his mouth lifting.

Talie shrugged, her smile turning playful. "Rebecca always has a knack for dragging us into her chaotic plans—whether it's drinking binges or strip club outings. She thinks it's the cure for everything."

Jesse raised an eyebrow, his gaze sharpening at the mention of strip clubs. "So," he murmured, his lips brushing against the curve of her neck, "I was your antidote?"

Heat bloomed under her skin, his touch igniting something that simmered just below the surface. Her breath hitched, hands reaching for him, tangling in his hair. But as his familiar scent enveloped her, something stirred—a memory buried deep but unmistakable. She inhaled sharply, her voice softening. "That perfume… it's the same one you wore at Club Viator."

Jesse paused, his expression unreadable for a brief moment. "Yes," he said simply.

Her stomach twisted, unease threading through her. "Did you go back to performing?" she asked, the question cautious, laced with apprehension.

He held her gaze, his silence stretching before he finally nodded. "I met the owner of a new club. He hired me on the spot."

Talie studied him, her emotions a tangled web of understanding, hurt, and something she couldn't quite name. "This is what I do best," Jesse said, his voice quieter now, as if the admission cost him something.

"I know," she whispered, lowering her gaze. His hand reached out, brushing gently against her cheek. His touch was tender but carried the weight of their shared past and unspoken fears.

"It's a good place. Same rules as Club Viator, same kind of clientele."

Her lips pressed into a thin line, her heart tightening. "A clientele of lost girls seeking the miracle antidote to make them lose their minds," she murmured, the unflattering truth of strip clubs hanging heavily between them, her words tinged with bitterness.

Jesse stayed silent, his eyes fixed on her, her words lingering in the space between them. She regretted them instantly, the tension unraveling the fragile thread of peace they had been holding onto.

"I'm crazy about you, Talie," he finally said, his voice low but filled with conviction. He leaned closer, his piercing blue eyes searching hers, as if willing her to see the truth in them.

Her throat tightened, fear rising to the surface. "I'm scared," she confessed, her voice barely a whisper.

Jesse's gaze softened, his intensity giving way to a warmth that wrapped around her like a quiet embrace. He leaned in, his unhurried approach thickening the air between them with anticipation. When their lips finally met, the kiss was tender, a gentle exploration that spoke of trust and unspoken promises. His lips lingered on hers like a soft breeze stirring something deep within her soul.

Their bodies nestled close, fingers tracing each other's skin with featherlight touches. Each caress was a silent declaration of what words couldn't express. The world beyond faded into nothingness, leaving only the warmth of their intimacy, a cocoon woven from their shared desire and connection.

The soft chirping of morning birds coaxed Talie from the lingering haze of bliss. Sunlight spilled through the curtains in golden streaks, casting a warm glow across the room. Jesse was in the shower, the soothing hum of water filling the quiet. She stretched languidly before stepping onto the balcony, craving the fresh morning air.

The city unfolded before her, its skyline bathed in morning sun. A gentle breeze teased her hair, brushing against her skin as she inhaled deeply, savoring the tranquility of the moment. Yet beneath the serenity, her heart whispered warnings. Love this consuming had the power to break her. The ghosts of past heartbreak stirred, a subtle ache she couldn't entirely shake.

The faint click of the door broke her reverie. Turning, she found Jesse stepping onto the balcony, his presence magnetic even in its simplicity. Sunlight painted his bare form in gilded hues, tracing every ridge and hollow of his body. Wordlessly, he crossed the space to her, his arms encircling her waist and pulling her close. His lips brushed against her neck, warm breath trailing over her skin while he murmured softly.

He settled into the chair behind him, pulling her onto his lap with an ease that made her feel weightless. His piercing blue eyes found hers, a perfect storm of intensity and devotion. Slowly, his fingers moved to the tie of her robe, loosening it with a careful precision that made her pulse quicken. The silk slipped away like water, baring her to the cool caress of the morning air. A shiver raced down her spine as his lips pressed softly against the curve of her breast, igniting a fire that chased away every shadow of doubt.

Lifting her, he aligned their bodies with an intimacy that felt as natural as breathing.

"Good morning," he murmured, his voice a low vibration that rumbled against her chest.

She smirked, her eyes darting toward the neighboring balconies. "Jesse, we're not exactly alone out here."

His lips curved into a devilish grin, his hands trailing possessive patterns down her back. "All the better," he murmured. "Let's give them a show they won't forget."

The rest of the morning unfolded like a dream. Jesse kept his promise, weaving pleasure into every moment until Talie felt the delicious ache of their reunion in every limb.

"So, do you have the day off?" he asked, popping a cherry into his mouth.

Talie nodded, feeling a wave of contentment wash over her. "Today and tomorrow, actually," she replied, her gaze drifting to the tray of fruit resting on the bed.

"Two days?" His voice dipped, a seductive playfulness creeping into his tone. "That's dangerous."

"And you?" she asked, tilting her head curiously, trying not to be swayed by the glint in his eyes.

"I work tonight. Tomorrow, I'm all yours," he said, his gaze steady, a playful challenge glinting in his eyes, daring her to make plans.

Her heart fluttered, but she kept her expression casual as she set her plate aside. "What's the place called?" she asked, keeping her voice light.

"The Tux, on McGill near Sainte-Catherine."

Talie leaned back against the headboard, processing his words. "Nice area," she murmured, her thoughts spinning.

Jesse nodded, watching her reaction carefully. "Yeah. It's pretty upscale. An associate of Diego's mentioned they were looking for performers."

Talie's brows knit together as she studied him. "Is the place run by Diego's crew?"

"No," he said quickly, pausing just long enough to let the word sink in. "And everything with them is settled now. I've got my new papers, my new identity. The rest… it's up to me. To us." His words carried a finality that made her chest tighten.

For a long moment, they simply looked at each other, the gravity of his situation pressing down on them both. Jesse set his plate aside and leaned in closer. "They didn't hesitate to tell me they'd put a bullet in my head if I talked."

Talie's breath caught. "I've been thinking about it constantly. I was terrified you wouldn't come back. It was unbearable," she confessed, her voice trembling with emotion. "I can't hold it all inside anymore. I need to tell

Rebecca. She's the one person who's always been there for me, no matter what. I can't keep lying to her."

Jesse's jaw tensed, and for a moment, he looked away. "Talie, every time we bring someone else into this, we take a risk."

"But she's different," Talie pressed, her voice firm with unwavering conviction. "I trust her with my life—and with yours."

The memory of nights spent confiding in Rebecca flooded back—how her friend had stood by her when they'd suspected her ex of cheating. Rebecca had kept every secret, even under pressure.

Jesse's intense gaze brought her back to the present. "If you trust her that much, then I trust you."

Relief washed over her, and she leaned in, resting her forehead against his. "I don't want to lose you."

She kissed him softly, letting the sweetness of his lips linger against hers. Her fingers tangled in his dark hair, stroking the fine strands at the nape of his neck. Jesse's strong hands pulled her closer until she was straddling him, her body molding to his. Her fingertips traced the firm lines of his side before she pressed gentle, adoring kisses to his chest. With a playful glint in her eyes, she looked up and teased, "So… does this new life mean my lover gets a new name too?"

Jesse smirked, his hips shifting slightly beneath her, letting her feel the desire building between them. "Derek Watson."

She laughed softly. "Derek Watson, huh?"

In one swift motion, Jesse flipped her onto her back, his hands pinning her wrists to the mattress. His grin turned wicked, his voice dipping into a dangerous, velvety tone. "You'll regret laughing at me," he growled, his blue eyes gleaming with mischief.

Her laughter faltered, replaced by breathless anticipation as he leaned closer, his lips brushing against her ear. "And when I'm done with you, you'll never forget my name."

That look—she knew it all too well. Whenever his smile curved like that, it always meant one thing: she was in for something unforgettable. The last time he'd worn that expression, she could barely walk for days—but every second had been worth it.

Ten

"Will you have enough energy to perform tonight?" Talie asked, her cheek resting against Jesse's biceps as they lay side by side, their bodies languid and entwined.

"I've got a battery that never runs out. Didn't you know?" he murmured, his fingers drawing lazy, feather-light circles on the small of her back.

She chuckled softly, her gaze flicking to the clock. The faint ache in her muscles served as a delicious reminder of the hours they'd spent tangled together. The sunlight had shifted across their skin from dawn to dusk, leaving them bathed in a warm, golden glow.

"'Live on love and fresh water' doesn't really suit you," she teased, sliding out of bed with a graceful stretch. "We need something better. How about 'live on sex and… more sex'?"

Jesse's laughter rang out, deep and rich, filling the room as his eyes tracked her every move. She swayed her hips playfully on her way to the bathroom, casting him a knowing glance over her shoulder. His gaze, warm and magnetic, clung to her until she disappeared behind the door.

The shower's hot spray was a soothing balm, easing the soreness that had settled deep in her muscles. She'd lost count of how many times they'd made love over the past two days, her body pushed to its limits yet still yearning for him.

"Are you going out tonight?" Jesse's voice drifted into the bathroom, casual but threaded with curiosity, cutting through the hiss of water.

"No," she called back, rinsing the last of the shampoo from her hair. "I need to relax, Mr. Don Juan."

She stepped out moments later, a towel wrapped snugly around her, water still glistening on her skin as her damp hair spilled over her shoulders. Jesse was leaning against the wall, his arms crossed over his chest, the pose accentuating the taut strength of his forearms and the corded muscles of his shoulders.

"Come over here," he said softly, his voice a low, enticing drawl. His gaze roamed her from head to toe, heating every inch it touched. "Let's see if I can help you… relax."

The apartment was silent after Jesse left for work. Talie decided to push through her fatigue with a quick workout. She had always been mindful of her figure, but since meeting Jesse, her insecurities had only grown sharper, her mind clouded with images of the glamorous women he encountered nightly.

When the workout was done, she showered again, exhaustion finally catching up with her as she sank into the couch. Her thoughts inevitably drifted back to him, the same way they had so many nights before. Around four in the morning, the soft click of the door closing stirred her awake. Jesse's quiet steps crossed the room, his hands slipping under her to lift her gently.

Her eyes fluttered open, her voice a sleepy whisper. "Hi."

"I didn't mean to wake you," he said, brushing a strand of hair from her face. His expression softened as she sat up, her green eyes meeting his, still hazy from sleep.

"I was waiting for you. Did you have a good evening?"

"Yes."

"And the clients?"

"A busy Saturday," he said, his eyes searching hers.

Talie tried to mask the pang of discomfort rippling through her chest. Her fingers ran absently through her long hair, letting it cascade to one side and exposing the curve of her neck. The gesture was instinctive, not meant to seduce, yet Jesse's gaze lingered. He caught the flicker of distance in her eyes, a chasm widening between them. It wasn't jealousy—what he saw ran deeper. She wasn't battling the women who lusted after him at the club; she was fighting her own thoughts, caught in a storm of inner conflict that he couldn't quite reach.

"You don't have to do this," he said softly, his gaze never wavering.

"Do what?" she asked, though she already knew the answer.

"Ask about my night, about the women. Wait up for me when you could be sleeping in a warm bed." Jesse's hand reached for hers. "I can tell it's not what your heart wants—knowing about the private dances, about the clients… I don't want you hurting yourself with this. If it didn't bother you, I'd tell you everything. But it does."

Her gaze dropped to the tattoo on his arm, her fingers tracing its lines as if searching for clarity. A heavy sigh escaped her lips.

"You're probably right," she admitted, her voice quiet. "The less I know, the easier it'll be."

He leaned in, brushing his lips against hers, the warmth of his breath dissolving the tension that hung between them. "No matter what I was doing tonight, you were the only thing on my mind," he murmured, his voice raw with sincerity.

Her breath hitched as his scent enveloped her, intoxicating and achingly familiar. Her hands slipped under his shirt, exploring the contours of his chest, her touch setting off sparks between them. Slowly, he unbuttoned her lilac blouse, revealing the soft curve of her breasts framed by delicate mauve lace.

His lips found her collarbone, traveling upward to her neck and ear, each kiss leaving a trail of fire in its wake. His voice dropped to a husky whisper, brushing against her skin. "I take back what I said. Waiting for me was the best decision you've ever made," he murmured, his teeth catching the delicate straps of her bra.

Talie let out a soft laugh, her fingers threading into his dark hair. The teasing heat of his touch sent ripples of excitement through her, momentarily dulling the lingering soreness in her body.

"Jesse," she breathed as he began to slide her skirt over her hips. "That area is… a little tender right now."

He froze, concern furrowing his brow. "Did I hurt you?"

She ran her tongue over her bottom lip, her cheeks flushing. It felt ridiculous to admit it, but physically, she really needed a break. "It's just… my body's never been through so much in such a short time."

His expression melted into one of gentle understanding, his hands gliding back up her thighs to adjust her skirt into place. "Then I'll focus on the rest of you," he said, his lips curving into a playful smirk before pressing a reverent kiss to the curve of her breast. Without missing a beat, he scooped her into his arms, cradling her with ease as he carried her toward the bedroom.

As she did every morning, Talie stepped onto the balcony, craving the warmth of the sun on her skin. But today, a brisk wind whipped against her, forcing her back inside. Wrapping her arms around herself, she cast a glance at the streets below. Passersby moved briskly, bundled in woolen jackets as the chill signaled the season's inevitable shift.

"Hey, gorgeous," Jesse's voice cut through her wandering thoughts. Turning, she spotted him leaning against the doorframe, exuding casual confidence. Keys dangled from his fingers, their faint jingle matching the playful glint in his eyes. "Come with me."

Her curiosity piqued, she slid her fingers into his. Tilting her head, she asked, "What are you up to now?"

"Just trust me. I want to show you something," he replied, tugging her gently toward the hallway.

The crisp air outside greeted them as they walked down the street, Jesse's stride confident and sure. His calm demeanor stood in stark contrast to her mind, which raced with curiosity. As they turned down a quiet side street, Talie's breath hitched at the sight ahead of them—a sleek, all-black sports car gleaming under the muted light. Its polished curves radiated sophistication, the very definition of luxury.

Jesse stopped beside the car and turned to her, his expression proud yet subdued. "What do you think?"

"Black is definitely your new color," she murmured, running her hand over the smooth, cool metal.

"It's an Aston Martin."

"For someone who's trying to stay under the radar, this isn't exactly subtle," she teased, sliding into the passenger seat.

Inside, the interior was a seamless blend of elegance and power. Her fingers brushed against the soft black leather, and for a fleeting moment, she thought of the bold red of his Maserati.

"What happened to the Maserati?" she asked, confusion coloring her voice, trying to piece it together.

He shrugged, his grip on the steering wheel firm but unbothered. "Gone. That's what happens when you leave an expensive car in a dark alley."

Talie's brows knit together as she studied his calm, almost too-relaxed expression. "You don't seem worried at all."

"It was part of the plan. No surprises here," he replied simply, his gaze focused on the road ahead while the car purred to life.

A quiet sigh escaped her lips as the reality of his situation settled over her. This life—his constant reinvention, his quiet resilience—was far from ordinary. Yet he carried it all with a calm that bordered on poetic.

"You've got an unshakable optimism."

"You have to keep moving forward," he said, his voice steady and thoughtful. "No matter how heavy the weight on your shoulders feels."

Her gaze dropped to her hands resting in her lap, his words echoing in the quiet spaces of her mind. She tried to imagine herself in his shoes, but the mere thought left her overwhelmed. *Maybe I just don't have enough faith*, she wondered.

"Are you religious?" she asked, her voice hesitant, unsure if the question would tread on delicate ground.

A faint smile curved his lips as he glanced at her. "Not in the traditional sense. I don't follow any religion, but I believe in something greater—a force that helps us achieve what we desire. Grace was the one who taught me that."

"I really want to have a serious conversation with her."

He nodded. "You will. But first, you're coming back to the orchard with me." His blue eyes met hers, locking her in place with their intensity.

His hand slid onto her thigh, the warmth of his touch sending a pleasant shiver up her spine before he returned his focus to the road. Her mind drifted to the memories they'd made together, replaying them like a film. She remembered the first time they'd met, the magnetic pull she felt toward him, and how hard she'd fought to resist. Their first kiss, their first night together, and all the intimate moments that followed—it all came flooding back, and she realized just how deeply she had fallen for him.

"Lost in your thoughts?" he asked, his voice low. "What are you thinking about?"

"Us," she said, her voice carrying a quiet warmth, as if the single word held a world of meaning.

"And what kind of thoughts?" he teased, his hand sliding a little higher on her thigh.

"Beautiful ones... pure ones," she said, the sparkle in her eyes giving away her mischief.

"Oh," he said, pretending to be disappointed.

"I was thinking about how we met," she continued, her tone softening, "and everything that's happened since."

"About my patience and persistence finally paying off..."

"Your patience and persistence that worked in my favor, you mean," she corrected, her voice light with laughter.

As they drove through the charming neighborhood, the stately homes stood proudly behind their manicured lawns. Sunlight filtered between the trees, casting golden rays that danced on the road. The scene felt magical, as if time itself had paused to bask in its beauty.

"Have you been to your new house yet?" Talie asked.

"I stopped by earlier this week. Made a few tweaks to the interior, minor stuff. And I put in a special order just for you."

"What?"

"You'll see," he said, his voice dripping with mystery.

Talie tilted her head, her lips curving into a playful smirk. "And how long are you planning to lie low as... Derek?"

she asked, the name slipping from her tongue with just the right touch of mockery.

Her mind flashed to their last fiery encounter, and a subtle warmth spread from her chest downward, leaving her cheeks faintly flushed.

"We're talking years," he said quietly, glancing at her as if to gauge her reaction.

The word hit her like a distant echo, reverberating painfully in her chest. Years. The idea of burying their joy, their love, under layers of secrecy for so long gnawed at her. The silence between them stretched, not heavy, but raw with unspoken questions.

The car rounded a gentle curve, sunlight flaring briefly and blindingly through the windshield. Jesse slowed the car and pulled onto a peaceful street. "And here we are," he said, parking in front of a breathtaking Spanish-style mansion.

Talie's eyes widened as she took in the stunning architecture—Tosca arches and grand columns that exuded timeless elegance. "Wow," she said, awe lacing her voice.

The street was lined with estates that seemed to compete for grandeur, each one whispering of wealth and privilege. It felt like stepping into a dream. *This must be what it's like to live among the rich and famous*, she thought.

As they continued walking, her gaze was drawn to a grand fountain, where koi fish glided gracefully beneath the shimmering surface. Jesse came to a stop beside her, mesmerized by the scene. His fingers absently grazed the stubble along his sharp jawline, lost in thought.

Talie's attention shifted to him, unable to look away. The soft light played across his form, catching on the curve of his jaw and the broad line of his shoulders. His gray-and-blue sweater clung to his frame, hinting at the power beneath.

Then, as if sensing her gaze, he looked up. A few unruly strands of hair fell across his forehead, and the smile that tugged at his lips was enough to melt away the chill in the air. It was the kind of smile that lit up her world, no matter how dim things seemed. Without a word, he reached for her, pulling her close, his lips capturing hers in a deep, lingering kiss.

"I love seeing that spark in your eyes. It's a shame you need rest," he whispered, leading her toward the entrance.

Inside, the mansion revealed itself as an elegant masterpiece. Every room exuded a harmonious blend of modern design, with rich wood and chrome accents complemented by vibrant artwork on the walls and ceilings. Talie's expression shifted into one of complete amazement as her eyes fell on the kitchen. At its center stood a massive island, its surface gleaming with the rich, intricate beauty of Jerusalem stone. She stepped closer, her fingers gently tracing the tiny fossils embedded in the stone, their patterns captivating her.

Jesse moved in behind her, his gaze drawn not just to the stone, but to her. "It's from Jerusalem, near the Dead Sea."

"Beautiful."

"It'd be even more beautiful with you on it," he murmured, his voice dropping to a husky, intimate tone.

The way he looked at her was electrifying, a raw intensity that seemed to burn straight through her, leaving her breathless. Before she could find her voice, he lifted her onto the countertop. The cold stone kissed her skin, a sharp contrast to the fire sparking between them as he stepped closer, his body filling the space between her legs. Her fingers curled against his broad shoulders for balance, her breath hitching under the weight of his presence.

"You don't even know what you do to me," he murmured, his words a caress against her skin as his fingers slipped beneath her lace panties.

Her lips parted on a soft sigh, and in that moment, he caught her bottom lip between his teeth. Her hips tilted toward him instinctively, her body silently pleading for more.

"To hell with rest," she whispered.

His eyes darkened with hunger as he unbuttoned his pants, the sight of Talie perched seductively on the sleek countertop only heightening his desire.

She watched him with parted lips, her breath shallow, her body thrumming with need. When he moved her panties aside and stepped between her thighs, the deliberate, unhurried pressure of his entry stole the air from her lungs. A long, trembling moan escaped her lips as he began to move, his rhythm slow at first, savoring every second of their connection.

The feel of her body writhing in pleasure beneath him drove him to push further. His rhythm grew more intense, each thrust pushing them closer to the edge. Talie met him at every beat, her legs tightening around his hips, her nails raking across his back in desperate, unrestrained passion.

Time became irrelevant as they lost themselves in each other, their bodies a perfect rhythm of rising heat and unspoken need. Every sigh that escaped her lips fueled his determination, every arch of her body only drawing him deeper. His movements grew more demanding, more consuming, driven by an insatiable hunger to see her unravel.

Their cries mingled, a raw symphony of passion echoing through the room, intensifying with each beat. Talie's body began to tremble, her breath shallow as the tension inside her wound tighter, coiling until it snapped. She shattered beneath him, her gasping cries breaking through the haze, wave after wave of pleasure surging over her.

But Jesse didn't stop. His relentless focus on her pushed her higher, his movements commanding her body to surrender completely. Her moans turned breathless, her mind fogged with sensation as another peak overtook her, her body trembling with the force of it.

When his release finally came, it was explosive, leaving him shaking as he collapsed against her. Their labored breaths filled the silence, bodies still tangled, clinging to the intensity of the moment.

He pulled her closer, his strong arms wrapping around her as if he couldn't bear to let her go. "I'll never get enough of you."

They finished touring the upstairs in fits of laughter, their exploration punctuated by stolen kisses and playful embraces. It felt like rediscovering a secret world of their own, one where time and responsibilities ceased to exist.

Jesse eventually led her to the basement, guiding her toward a secluded section. Talie stepped forward, curiosity lighting her features, but the moment she spotted the bright red sofa and the polished dance pole in front of it, she burst into laughter.

"Planning to rehearse your performances down here?" she teased, turning to face him.

"It's not for me," he replied, pulling her onto the plush cushions beside him. "I saw you at the club. Let's just say, I wanted that exclusivity right here, where I can enjoy it all to myself."

"You might be waiting a long time," she quipped, her laughter softened the edge of her words.

"With you," he whispered, his lips grazing her ear, "everything's worth the wait." His lips trailed heat down her neck, and her protests dissolved into a quiet gasp as he worked his magic.

Her fingers found their way to his back, nails tracing light patterns across his skin before sliding lower to rest on the firm curve of his ass. He groaned in approval, his voice carrying a note of amused reprimand.

"I love that," he murmured, his breath hot against her skin, "but if you keep it up, I'm going to need another excuse to cover the scratches."

Her cheeks flushed, her laughter turning sheepish as she recalled the marks she'd left on his back.

"I had to keep it covered at the Tux," he said, his grin teasing.

Her hands flew to her face in mock embarrassment, muffling her laugh.

He nodded toward the dance pole with a mischievous glint in his eye. "I suppose you'll find a way to make it up to me."

After several attempts to coax her into a performance, Jesse finally led her outside. The moment she stepped into the open air, the breathtaking view made her forget everything else. A vast, shimmering pool stretched out before her, its surface kissed by sunlight and fed by a cascading waterfall that tumbled gracefully into the water. Surrounding it, hundreds of vibrant flowers bloomed in a riot of colors, creating an otherworldly backdrop. It felt like a slice of paradise carved into the earth, untouched and eternal.

"This place is unreal," she said, genuinely impressed. "Was your last house anything like this?"

He leaned casually against a silver maple, his arms crossed as he watched her take it all in. "More or less," he said with a shrug, the faint smile tugging at his lips betraying his pride

"I'm going to feel like my apartment's a shoebox after this!"

"You're welcome anytime," he said, his tone carrying a warmth that made her feel how much he would truly enjoy having her there, no matter the time of day.

She smiled as they wandered toward a hammock strung between two towering trees, their steps silent on the lush grass. Talie soaked in the opulence surrounding them, but a troubling thought crept into her mind—she couldn't help but wonder about the darker truths hidden beneath the surface of such luxury. A pang of discomfort twisted in her chest, breaking the spell of the moment.

"Did you ever see anything illegal at Club Viator?" she asked quietly, her voice heavy with unease.

"Of course."

"And that didn't make you want to leave? To find something else?" she pressed, her brow furrowing slightly.

He turned to face her, a flicker of something unreadable crossing his face before he spoke. "No," he said simply. "It was the start of my career, and I was in a dark place. Back then, danger thrilled me just as much as sex did… if that gives you any idea of who I used to be."

She studied him in silence, her heart aching for the man he had been. "I'm glad I didn't know you back then."

"Me too. I would've ruined everything," he said as he reached out, pulling her closer to taste her lips. It was soft at first, almost reverent, before deepening into something more.

"You're so attentive," she whispered against his lips, "The caresses, the kisses, the way you look at me… You're incredible."

"And yet, I wasn't always this way," he murmured, his eyes darkening with the weight of old memories. "I wasn't balanced. I was selfish. A real narcissist."

"I can't imagine you like that."

He smiled, but a shadow flickered in his azure eyes, a reminder of the past that would always linger in him. Those memories were etched deep into his soul, destined to remain forever. Lost in thought, he pressed his lips to the hollow of her neck, lingering on the softness of her skin.

As the evening breeze rustled the leaves above, they held each other close, finding comfort in their shared warmth. The world around them faded, leaving only the gentle sway of the hammock and the quiet whispers of the wind.

Eleven

The calm atmosphere of the agency enveloped Talie as she walked in, her heels clicking softly against the polished floors. Rebecca's voice called out from across the room, cheerful and teasing.

"You left so early on Friday!" she exclaimed, her hands busy sorting through a stack of client folders.

Talie glanced up, a faint smile curving her lips. "I know, but I was so exhausted. How did your night turn out?"

Rebecca rolled her eyes with a laugh, shaking her head as she leaned against her desk. "You have no idea. David got completely drunk and passed out on my couch."

"And Josh?"

"He left not long after you did. He even said he's eager to see you again."

Talie raised an eyebrow, feigning nonchalance. "Clearly, he didn't notice me ignoring him all evening."

Rebecca smirked, twirling a lock of her hair. "Or maybe he's just persistent."

Persistence, what an intriguing topic, Talie thought, recalling Jesse's unrelenting pursuit of her. Weeks of quiet persistence, until his presence became impossible to ignore. No one could match that kind of determination.

"And the girls?" she asked, steering the conversation to safer ground. "Did they meet anyone interesting?"

Rebecca shook her head. "Not really. But speaking of the girls, did you hear they went to this new club in town? It's called the Tux. Apparently, it's even better than Club Viator!" Her eyes sparkled with excitement.

The mention of the club made Talie's heart seize. A sudden tightness coiled in her stomach, and she forced a neutral expression. The conversation she had been avoiding was now staring her in the face. This wasn't how she had planned to bring it up, but Rebecca deserved the truth.

"Yes… I've heard of it," she replied cautiously, her voice steady despite the storm brewing inside her.

Rebecca leaned forward. "The girls said the shows were insane! Way more intense than anything they've ever seen!"

Talie's composure wavered, her hands gripping the edge of the chair. "Jesse works there," she blurted, the words tumbling out before she could stop them.

Rebecca froze, her excitement replaced by confusion. "What?"

"He never went abroad, Becca," she confessed, her words thick with emotion.

Rebecca's eyes widened in shock, her disbelief clear. "Are you serious?"

She nodded, her voice trembling. "But no one can know he's still in Montreal. You understand?"

Rebecca's jaw slackened, her thoughts visibly racing. "Wait, what? How? What happened?"

"He… he changed his identity so he could stay here," she whispered, her green eyes shimmering with unshed tears.

"And no one suspects a thing?" Rebecca asked, still trying to process the information.

"I don't think so," she murmured, guilt washing over her. "Jesse wasn't happy about me telling you, but I couldn't live in this lie anymore. I'm so scared, Becca."

Rebecca's face shifted from confusion to deep concern. "Oh my God… this is a lot."

"I know," she whispered, her voice breaking. She reached for Rebecca's hand, her desperation spilling over. "I couldn't keep it inside any longer. All week, I had no idea where he was. I didn't know if he was okay, if he needed me, if he was even alive. It was unbearable."

The words poured out of her, raw and unfiltered, as tears streaked her cheeks. Her breath hitched, the storm of emotions finally breaking free after days of suppression.

Rebecca whispered softly, pulling her friend into a comforting embrace. "Don't worry. I won't say a word."

Talie clung to her, her sobs muffled against her shoulder. "It feels like I'm never allowed simple happiness," she muttered, her voice barely audible through the tears.

Nestled in her friend's arms, she let everything out—her sorrow, her fear, her frustration. The heavy burden of keeping Jesse's secret finally lifted as she cried, allowing herself to feel the full weight of everything she had been carrying alone.

As she did every evening after work, Talie made her way to Jesse's mansion. The vast gym, where she tested her limits, and the massive TV, where she passed the time waiting for him to return, offered a semblance of comfort. Yet, despite its grandeur, the house often felt overwhelmingly large and hauntingly empty. The growing intimacy between them filled her with warmth, but the persistent sense of isolation clung to her like a shadow. The outside world—the one she had once thrived in—felt like a distant echo.

Every now and then, flashes of those carefree, wild nights would flood her thoughts. Rebecca, ever the loyal friend, would regale her with tales of their thrilling escapades, tempting her with the allure of freedom, nudging her back toward that familiar excitement.

Temptation, as always, had a way of weakening her resolve.

"I'm going out for a drink with Claudia and two of her friends," Rebecca said, tidying up her desk before leaving.

"Where to?" she asked, feigning casual interest.

"That pub near my place. Their cocktails are divine, and the crowd is fantastic. Want to come?"

The question lingered, pulling at something deep within her. For a moment, Talie felt a flicker of curiosity. "I haven't been out in a while," she said, the words coming out slower than she'd intended. "Maybe I could join you for a drink or two…"

Rebecca laughed, snapping her laptop shut with an air of triumph. "Or three! Come on, who are you kidding? You can't change human nature."

Talie smiled faintly, a small tug of longing curling in her chest. "I do miss our girls' nights out."

"I miss them too. But I get it. You're in a tough situation. It's not easy, juggling everything you've got on your plate."

Talie let out a heavy sigh. "I try not to dwell on it too much, or I'll drive myself crazy. You wouldn't believe how often the worry grips me. I keep imagining the worst—what if the police finally track him down?"

"You're carrying a lot on your shoulders, but you've got to stay positive. It's the only way to keep from losing yourself."

"My sanity?" she scoffed, the corner of her mouth twitching into a bitter smile as they stepped out of the office. "I think I lost that ages ago."

When she arrived at the mansion, the steady thump of music drifted up from the basement. It wasn't unusual—Jesse's workouts had become a near-ritual. She made her way toward the sound and leaned against the doorframe, her eyes drinking in the sight of him. Jesse was in the middle of a set, his athletic form moving with practiced precision, each ripple and line of his abs defined under the soft light. Noticing her, he flashed a dazzling smile and wiped his face with the towel draped over his shoulder.

"Hey, gorgeous," he called out, noticing her. His voice was low, rough from exertion. "How was your day?

She smiled faintly, trying to shake off the effect he had on her. "Chaotic. Everyone's losing their minds over the cold, planning trips to the South like it's the apocalypse."

He chuckled, running the towel over his face. "That sounds like a distraction we could use. Beats hearing about Rebecca's latest hookup stories."

"There's no escaping those, trust me."

He arched an eyebrow, his playful gaze narrowing on her. "And you—don't you share our steamy sessions with her?"

Her lips curved into a mischievous smirk. "Of course! You know me!"

The glint in his eyes darkened as he stepped closer, bridging the distance between them. "In that case," he murmured, his voice dropping an octave, "I guess I should give you some fresh material."

The tension in the air thickened, every inch of him radiating heat while he closed the distance between them. Her breath hitched when his lips brushed hers, igniting sparks along her skin. Just as she leaned into him, expecting him to deepen the kiss, he pulled back, the wicked curve of his smile promising more.

"You're so cruel!" she teased, biting her lower lip.

He traced a slow hand down her arm, his touch light as a whisper yet leaving heat in its wake. "Consider it payback for all the nights you made me work for it at the club."

Her arms looped around his neck, fingers threading through his damp hair, pulling him closer.

"You sure?" she said, her voice sultry, as she pressed herself against him, the soft curve of her breast grazing his torso. Her lips hovered over his, the promise of a kiss driving him wild.

Unable to resist her any longer, he gave in completely, his lips crashing into hers with unrestrained hunger. The air around them grew electric, charged with raw, unfiltered desire. His hands gripped her waist, pulling her against him with a force that left no room for doubt. He needed her— every inch, every touch, every soft sigh she gave him.

She gasped into his mouth, her fingers clutching at his shoulders before sliding down his chest, tracing the firm lines of his body. Her touch, confident and teasing, broke down the last remnants of his control. As her fingers slipped just beneath the waistband of his shorts, his groan rumbled against her lips, the sound dripping with surrender and need.

"I'm sorry I made it hard for you at the club," she whispered teasingly, her breath warm against his skin as her touch became bolder, stoking the fire between them.

"You've got an hour to make it up to me," he growled softly, the gleam in his eyes dangerous and intoxicating, bracing himself for the pleasure that awaited.

The downtown streets pulsed with energy, a chaotic symphony of honking horns and hurried footsteps weaving through the crowded sidewalks. Talie moved with confidence, her pace matching the city's electric rhythm, her friends flanking her in easy camaraderie. The noise, the rush—it all felt alive.

Then, as if orchestrated by the city itself, a sharp gust of wind cut through the street. It tugged at her miniskirt, sending it flying upward before she could react. A chorus of laughter erupted behind her, followed by a playful whistle.

"Woo!" someone called, catching sight of her lacy underwear. Heat flushed her cheeks, but she brushed off the comment with a sharp eye roll, gripping her skirt firmly against her thighs.

"I think it's time to retire the miniskirts for the season," Rebecca teased, giving her a playful swat on the butt.

"Becca!" Talie exclaimed, her voice tinged with exasperation as she shook her head.

"So, first time at the Tux?" Anna and Vivianne asked, curiosity lighting up her face.

"Yes."

"You're going to love it," Claudia said, her smile stretching across her face.

Talie glanced at Rebecca, her nerves bubbling just beneath the surface. "I can't believe you convinced me to come," she muttered under her breath.

"It'll do you more good than harm," Rebecca reassured her.

More good than harm? she thought. Watching Jesse, her Jesse, strip for other women? Harm. Seeing him simulate a steamy encounter with some voluptuous blonde whose hands wandered too freely? More harm. Witnessing him escort a client into the private lounge? Pure torture.

Yet here she was, knowing full well the mental anguish she was walking into. Despite it all, she couldn't douse the burning need to see how he behaved around other women. Curiosity and jealousy warred within her, their boundaries blurring until she could no longer tell where one ended and the other began.

As the sleek black facade of the Tux came into view, Talie's steps faltered. The building loomed ahead, radiating an aura of exclusivity. Impeccably dressed women clustered at the entrance, each one seemed effortlessly poised, like they belonged in the pages of a glossy magazine.

Viviane and Anna pushed ahead, their excitement spilling over in bright, animated chatter. Talie trailed behind, her nerves simmering. How would Jesse react when he saw her?

"I don't remember the last time we stood in line," Rebecca mused, eyeing the women ahead of them.

"This place is worth it," Viviane gushed. "The dancers are classier, the shows are insane, and the vibe? Totally unmatched."

Anna adjusted the straps of her dress, her smile growing wider with anticipation. "I'm going all out tonight."

Talie swallowed hard, wishing she could share their enthusiasm. Instead, her gaze drifted to the doorman, who admitted clients one by one with a swift nod, his expression unreadable.

"I wish Tristan worked here," Claudia sighed.

As the line inched forward, Talie tried to steady her nerves. Jesse's appearance might have changed, but those unmistakable, intense eyes would give him away.

"Enjoy your evening," the doorman greeted, his low, resonant voice carrying a note of formality as he stepped aside, letting them through.

Excited, Anna and Viviane hurried ahead, claiming a table with an eagerness that contrasted sharply with Talie's growing anxiety. The others followed, settling in to take in the club's lavish interior. The space oozed decadence—plush velvet seating, dim lighting that hinted at mystery, and the faint scent of expensive cologne in the air. The venue was nearly full, clients already nursing drinks as they exchanged casual flirtations with the dancers scattered like stars across the room.

Talie forced a breath, her gaze darting between the tables and the raised stage. Relief washed over her when she didn't immediately spot Jesse. But the reprieve was fleeting. She knew it wouldn't last.

"Want a drink?" Rebecca offered, tapping her thigh encouragingly.

"Something light," she replied, doing her best to mask the nervous flutters in her stomach.

"I can't wait for you to see my favorite dancer," Viviane exclaimed, brimming with excitement.

Talie's stomach twisted at the thought. What if Jesse was the star Viviane was raving about? The knot in her chest tightened, her breath growing shallow as the possibility loomed.

"No sign of Tristan," Claudia muttered, disappointment creeping into her voice.

"That's no great loss," Rebecca whispered in Talie's ear.

Suddenly, the room plunged into darkness, and the hushed murmur of voices transformed into excited whispers. A dramatic shift in the lighting cast an ethereal glow over the stage, and a loud roar pierced the air. A sleek motorcycle rolled into view, ridden by a man clad in black leather.

Talie's breath caught as the helmet was removed, revealing tousled dark hair framing a chiseled face she knew all too well. Jesse.

The crowd erupted into cheers the moment he shrugged off his leather jacket, revealing the sculpted lines of his torso. His smirk was magnetic, pulling everyone into his orbit, moving in sync with the pounding bass.

"That's him!" Viviane exclaimed, nearly jumping out of her seat with excitement. Rebecca shot a quick glance at Talie, who sat frozen, her eyes locked on the stage where the scene unfolded.

"Are you okay?" she whispered.

"Not really."

Seeing her friend's distress, Rebecca didn't push further, instead turning her attention back to the stage. Jesse was in his element, commanding the crowd's adoration as he moved with sensuality. To the raucous delight of the audience, he tore off his leather pants, leaving only a pair of briefs that clung to him like a second skin. The cheers grew deafening when he gripped the pole, spinning with practiced ease and igniting a frenzy in the room.

When he stepped off the stage, he wove through the tables, stopping just a few meters from theirs. He extended his hand to a bachelorette in a veil and guided her onto the stage, seating her in a chair before launching into an even more provocative routine.

Despite the energy crackling through the room, Talie felt a growing weight in her chest. She repeated to herself that it was just a job, but the unease lingered. The simulated intimacy made her breath catch, but not in the way it once had.

"I feel like I'm the one getting hot over here," Viviane joked, fanning herself.

"He must be amazing in bed," Anna added with a sly grin, her eyes fixed on Jesse's every move.

"What a perfect ass," Viviane chimed in.

Talie bit her tongue, holding back a torrent of words that would have silenced them all. Stories that would have left them speechless, envious.

Noticing her friend's strained expression, Rebecca gave her arm a soft, reassuring stroke. "I'm sorry for dragging you here," she muttered, guilt creeping into her tone.

Claudia leaned closer, her concern cutting through the buzz of conversation. "Are you okay?" she asked, her eyes scanning her friend's face for any hint of reassurance.

"Yes, yes," she said weakly, pasting on a smile she hoped was convincing.

Anna's voice broke through, her excitement sharp and unapologetic. "I'm definitely getting a private dance with him tonight!" she announced, her eyes practically sparkling.

Viviane, riding on Anna's energy, added eagerly, "Me too!"

"What about you, girls?" Anna asked, her gaze sweeping around the table.

Claudia shrugged casually. "Not for me."

"Me neither," Rebecca said, glancing at her friend.

Anna's gaze landed on Talie, the unspoken challenge clear. "And you?" she pressed, leaning forward, her curiosity alive.

"Not tonight," Talie replied, avoiding their curious gazes.

As their chatter resumed, Jesse continued working the room, his magnetic presence commanding every woman's attention. He was busier here than she'd ever seen him at Club Viator, seamlessly transitioning between private dances and his performances. His schedule seemed impossibly packed, and yet he moved with ease, leaving a trail of breathless clients in his wake.

Impatience danced across Anna's features as she rose from her seat. With a calculated stride, she made her way to the stage, positioning herself near the edge. Her confidence radiated as she gestured toward their table, her intent impossible to ignore. Jesse's piercing gaze skimmed over them briefly, a fleeting glance that landed like a whisper before he returned to his routine.

Viviane sighed dreamily, breaking the moment. "He has an aphrodisiac scent, girls. And those piercing blue eyes…"

Claudia tilted her head, her gaze following his every move with quiet fascination. "He reminds me of Jesse."

The mention of his name sent an invisible jolt through the table. Both Rebecca and Talie tensed, their previously relaxed expressions turning guarded.

"Who's Jesse?" Viviane asked, intrigued.

"He's a former dancer from Club Viator," Claudia explained, throwing a sympathetic smile in her friend's direction.

Talie's hands clenched in her lap, her breath uneven. "He does look a lot like him," she said, her voice barely above a whisper, her eyes clouded with emotion.

Catching her friend's somber expression, Claudia let the comparison drop. But Anna, oblivious to Talie's internal struggle, remained fixated on Jesse, her excitement bubbling over with each seductive move he made. She commented enthusiastically on the reactions of the women he danced for, her voice rising with every cheer from the audience.

For a while, Talie clung to a growing sense of relief—Jesse hadn't come near their table. She kept her focus on anything but the stage, hoping to remain invisible in the crowd. But just as that thought settled in her mind, she noticed him stepping off the stage, his strides purposeful, his path unmistakable. He was heading toward their table.

Each step he took echoed in her chest, a relentless rhythm of inevitability. The room seemed to draw a collective breath, every woman's gaze magnetized to his. Confidence radiated off him in waves, his practiced smile lighting up the faces he passed, leaving them glowing. But for Talie, every step felt like an echo of something she wasn't ready to confront.

"He's coming!" Anna squealed, sitting up straighter and adjusting her cleavage with a coy grin.

Talie shifted in her seat, fighting the urge to hide. Her pulse quickened, anxiety flooding her veins. *What am I doing here?* She glanced at Rebecca, whose concerned gaze lingered on her. But there was no time to escape. Jesse had reached their table.

"Ladies," he greeted, his voice smooth as velvet, his lips brushing Anna's cheeks before turning his smoldering gaze to the rest of the group. He acknowledged each woman with practiced charm, but when his eyes landed on Talie, a flash of surprise flickered across his features. It disappeared almost instantly, replaced by a mask of cool composure.

"Good evening," he said, his tone seductive.

The music shifted, its bass deep and pulsing, wrapping around them like a heavy fog. He climbed onto a stool, his hair falling into his eyes in a way that cast shadows over his sharp features. The dim lighting played tricks, sharpening the edges of his face and making him appear untouchable. He began to move with the rhythm, his belt sliding free with a teasing slowness that drew gasps from the room.

Talie was frozen, her breath catching as memories rushed in unbidden. The way he moved, the way his body commanded attention—it was achingly familiar. Each sway of his hips sent ripples through her, a heady mix of longing and discomfort that left her dizzy.

Anna's flirtatious smiles grew bolder, her focus entirely on him, while Viviane sat wide-eyed, her excitement spilling over with every seductive move. Jesse's hand drifted lower, skimming his chest before disappearing beneath the waistband of his briefs. Gasps rippled through the crowd, but Talie barely noticed. In that moment, his gaze sought hers again. The connection was immediate, electric, and unrelenting. The air seemed to thicken, her spine tingling under the intensity of his stare.

Then, with a playful smirk, he broke the moment, shifting his focus back to Anna. In perfect sync with the music, he let his pants fall, the smooth fabric pooling at his feet. The room erupted with cheers, and Anna's gaze swept over him with unabashed appreciation. Talie forced herself to look away, her hands trembling against the table as she sought refuge in Rebecca's expression. She let out a shaky sigh, trying to steady herself.

When she dared to look back, his eyes found hers again, unwavering and heavy with something unspoken. Her stomach churned, guilt and longing tangling in a knot that threatened to unravel her. She looked away quickly, shame and confusion warring inside her as she fought to keep herself together.

As the song came to a sultry close, Anna leaned forward, planting a kiss on Jesse's cheek. Her hand lingered on his arm, her fingers tracing the sculpted lines of his muscles. Jesse acknowledged the others with a nod, his charm effortless, but his gaze lingered on Talie. The brief moment stretched between them, heavy and charged, before he turned away, leaving her reeling.

"I want him! I want him!" Anna exclaimed breathlessly, her eyes following him as he moved to another table.

"Too intense! What did I tell you?" Viviane chimed in, fanning herself dramatically, pretending the room had grown unbearably warm.

Anna leaned in, her tone shifting to something more serious. "Do you think he sleeps with his clients? Because I'm really tempted."

"Of course," Viviane replied confidently. "He probably has a different girl every night. He can have anyone he wants."

Talie's chest tightened, her pulse hammering in her ears. A surge of rage bubbled up inside her, threatening to break through the fragile grip she had on her emotions. Each casual remark felt like a dagger, twisting deeper until her resolve began to fray. Her hands clenched into fists under the table, fighting the overwhelming urge to lash out.

"I think I'm going to wait for him outside the club," Anna announced boldly, determination gleaming in her eyes.

The other girls turned to her, surprise flickering across their faces.

"You're serious?" Claudia asked, raising an eyebrow.

"I said I wanted to have a good time, and I meant it!"

A wave of realization hit Talie like a crashing tide—Anna's words mirrored the unspoken desires of most of the women in the club. Panic swelled in her chest, choking her with the terrifying thought that Jesse's clients might actually wait for him after his nights, harassing or seducing him. The image was suffocating.

Without a word, she pushed back her chair, her movements stiff and abrupt as she stood. The girls exchanged confused glances, watching her retreat into the crowd.

"I'll check on her," Claudia offered, concern etching her features.

"No," Rebecca said softly, placing a calming hand on her arm. "Let her have a moment. She needs it."

"Are you sure?"

"Yes. She just needs to blow off some steam."

To everyone's surprise, Talie reappeared only a few minutes later, her face steeled with resolve. She grabbed her blazer and slung it over her arm. "I'm leaving," she said flatly, her tone clipped and distant.

Rebecca's hand shot out instinctively. "Let me drive you."

"No, it's fine. I'll take a taxi."

"Talie, let me—"

"Becca, it's fine," she cut in, her green eyes flashing with a fiery intensity that silenced the table.

The tension hung heavy as she turned on her heels and strode toward the exit, her steps purposeful but shaky. She didn't glance back, didn't let herself think about Jesse, the club, or anything else. All she knew was that she needed to escape—needed space to breathe, to find some semblance of calm in the storm raging within her.

Her steps echoed against the quiet night, loud and rhythmic in the stillness. She didn't care where she was going, as long as it led her away from the suffocating tension of the club.

Her mind was a tempest of emotions. Self-loathing clawed at her for letting curiosity drag her into that place, into his world. Anger followed swiftly—white-hot and unrelenting—directed at the women in the club. She could still see them, perfect and predatory, their manicured nails tracing the lines of his body, treating him like he belonged to them. The thought made her stomach churn with disgust.

She clenched her teeth and shook her head violently, as if she could physically shake away the tormenting images. How could she ever compete with those stunning, young women? And what was she? A woman weighed down by doubts, fears, and insecurities, hopelessly vulnerable to the endless tide of women who would stop at nothing to have him.

The idea of Jesse growing tired of her gnawed at the edges of her sanity. She could see it so clearly—his piercing blue eyes wandering, drawn to the next inviting smile, the next perfect figure that promised excitement and novelty. The thought of losing him, of seeing him with someone else, was a knife to her chest, twisting deeper with every passing second.

The ache in her chest grew unbearable, her fears pressing down on her until it felt as if the night itself was conspiring to crush her.

Twelve

Lying in bed, her eyes wide open, Talie stared at the clock, each minute stretching on like an eternity. The apartment was cloaked in an unnerving stillness, amplifying the restless rhythm of her heart. She strained her ears, waiting for the sound of the front door opening, her breath shallow as tension coiled tightly within her. When the door finally clicked open, her chest constricted, her body tensing.

She closed her eyes, feigning a peaceful slumber, though the erratic heartbeat betrayed her facade. The sound of Jesse's quiet steps filled the room, sending a ripple of tension through her body. He slipped under the covers, the warmth of his frame pressing intimately against hers. Slowly, he swept her long hair aside, exposing the curve of her neck. His lips brushed her skin with delicate intent, his breath warm and unhurried. He lingered, attuned to the uneven cadence of her breathing, a silent testament to the emotions she tried to hide.

"I know you're not asleep, gorgeous," he whispered, his lips grazing her ear.

Her chest tightened. "I'm sorry," she breathed, her words barely audible. She didn't have to say more; the weight of her turmoil spoke volumes.

"There was nothing good waiting for you there tonight," he said gently, his tone laced with affection. "And you knew it."

"I was curious," she admitted, sitting up, her gaze falling to her lap.

Jesse exhaled softly, shifting beside her. "Curiosity can be dangerous when it hurts you," he replied.

The silence stretched between them, heavy with unspoken questions. Finally, she broke it, her voice trembling as she asked, "Do clients… do they wait for you after the club closes?"

Jesse met her gaze in the dim light, his fingers lovingly tracing circles on her skin. "Talie, asking these questions is only going to hurt you."

"I need to know," she insisted, her heart aching with uncertainty.

The vulnerability in her tone made him pause. "Sometimes," he admitted, his words measured, careful.

"Do they… leave you their numbers?" she pressed, the jagged edge of her question cutting into her resolve.

"Yes," he said softly.

Her breath hitched, and she looked away, unable to meet his gaze. "Jesse," she whispered, her voice breaking,

"How can I compete with that? With them? You could have anyone you want."

He reached out, his fingers tilting her chin up so their eyes met. "Stop. This isn't about them, Talie."

"There comes a day when you miss something, and it's not the object of your desire, it's the desire itself," she murmured, reciting the quote with melancholy.

"Jouhandeau wrote beautiful quotes, but he wasn't always right."

Her eyes filled with tears as the doubts came flooding to the surface. "I'm scared," she confessed, her voice trembling. "I can't help it."

Jesse rested his forehead against hers, his touch grounding her. "Stop feeding those fears," he said quietly. "Don't let them grow. Focus on us. On what's real."

Her breath came in shaky waves, absorbing his words, her hands gripping his wrist like a lifeline. "I want to believe you."

"Don't let tonight destroy what we have," he murmured, leaning in until his lips captured hers in a kiss that was tender yet grounding, as if he was trying to etch his devotion into her very soul. The delicate straps of her nightgown slipped down her shoulders, his fingers following their descent, leaving a trail of warmth along her skin.

When he pulled back, he held her gaze with an intensity that made her feel seen, completely and utterly. He hovered over her, his touch exploring her body with a yearning for closeness that went beyond mere physical need.

Talie's fingers roamed his muscular back, feeling the tension beneath his skin, but Jesse caught her arms, gently pinning them above her head. He smiled down at her, a playful glint in his eyes. She expected the passion between them to erupt, to consume them entirely, but instead, Jesse's touch remained achingly tender. Each caress, every whispered word, felt like a vow, as if he wanted her to feel the depth of his love in every lingering moment.

"You truly embodied the expression 'making love' tonight," she whispered, her voice hushed but steady as they lay side by side. "I could feel it in every touch."

"You'll believe me when I tell you I love you," he murmured, his words filled with quiet conviction.

Her lips curved into a soft smile, fingers threading through the untamed strands of his hair. And as sleep finally claimed her, the shadows of doubt faded, replaced by the warmth of his arms and the certainty of his love.

"Last night at the Tux really shook you up, didn't it?" Rebecca remarked, her sharp eyes catching her friend absently flipping through a cruise catalog on her desk.

"More than I thought it would," Talie admitted, her words barely above a whisper.

"And what did Jesse say when he got back?"

"He said it wasn't a good idea," she replied, her voice tinged with regret. "And he was right."

"You know what? It probably hit harder because Claudia's friends were talking about him. If they'd been gushing over someone else, it wouldn't have felt so personal."

Talie managed a small, vulnerable smile. "You're probably right," she conceded, pushing the catalog aside and rising to grab a bottle of water. The moment she turned toward the kitchen, the sound of the agency's door opening drew her attention.

They both looked up, their surprise mirrored in each other's faces as Clayton stepped inside. Dressed casually in athletic pants and a fitted shirt, his easy confidence filled the room. "Hey," he greeted, his tone warm but serious.

"Hey," they responded in unison.

"Talie," he said, taking a step closer, "can we talk for a minute?"

She hesitated, a flicker of unease stirring inside her. "Uh…sure," she replied cautiously.

"Outside?" he suggested, his voice low, as if the walls themselves were listening.

Talie's nerves flared, but she nodded. "Okay."

He offered Rebecca a polite smile before holding the door open for Talie. She followed him outside, the cool air brushing against her skin as he leaned against a concrete block. He crossed his arms, his expression earnest, yet there was an undercurrent of tension she couldn't ignore.

"I wanted to talk about Jesse," he began, cutting straight to the point. "I know he can't really talk right now, but I was hoping you'd keep me in the loop."

Talie blinked, her thoughts racing as she tried to gauge how much he knew—and how much she should reveal. His concern seemed genuine, but there was something in his tone that put her on edge.

"Is he okay?" he asked.

"Yes," she said cautiously, her voice steady despite the knot forming in her stomach.

Relief flickered across his face, but his gaze didn't soften. "Good. I need to meet with him. Somewhere private, discreet. It's important."

Her brows furrowed, uncertainty threading through her voice. "This sounds serious."

"It is." He held out his hand. "Let me put my number in your phone. I'll wait for the information."

She hesitated for only a moment before handing it over, watching as he typed his contact information. When he returned the phone to her, his demeanor softened.

"You know," he said, "when Jesse took you home from the club that night, I could tell there was something real between you two."

His words disarmed her, warming her cheeks even as her stomach twisted with uncertainty. But she kept her lips pressed together, unsure of how to respond.

"I'll be waiting for your message," he said, leaning in. He kissed her on both cheeks, then turned and walked away without a backward glance.

Talie remained rooted to the spot, the conversation pressing heavily on her chest. Was Jesse in trouble?

She exhaled slowly, forcing her feet to move as she made her way back into the agency. Her steps felt heavier than before, her thoughts a tangled mess. Pushing open the agency door, she found Rebecca waiting for her, arms crossed, her head tilted in a way that betrayed her curiosity. "What was that about?"

"He needs to talk to Jesse about something important," she said, her voice trailing off as if the words were meant more for herself than her friend.

Rebecca straightened, her curiosity morphing into unease. He knows he's in Montreal?"

"Looks like it."

"Do you think Jesse's in some kind of trouble? she pressed, her voice dropping.

"I don't know. But whatever it is, it seems big."

Throughout the day, Talie's unease festered with every unanswered call to Jesse. By the time she locked up the agency, her worry had taken root, its weight impossible to ignore. Her mind offered no alternatives—she had to see him.

"Jesse?" she called out, her voice slicing through the stillness of the grand entryway of his mansion. The echo that greeted her only heightened her nerves.

Descending the steps, she found him in his gym, his body a vision of strength as he finished a set of pull-ups. His toned frame glistened with sweat under the muted light, and his expression softened the moment he saw her.

"Hey," he greeted, his deep voice warm, but concern flickered in his eyes as he caught the unease etched into her features. His smile faltered. "What's wrong?"

"Clayton came to the agency today," she blurted, her words tumbling out in a rush.

Jesse froze, his brows pulling together in sharp surprise. "What?"

"He said he needs you to set up a meeting place. Apparently, he has something important to tell you."

He raked a hand through his damp hair, his expression growing more serious. "Did he say why?"

"No," she admitted, watching the tension build in his posture. "But he seemed… I don't know, worried."

His jaw tightened, the sharp angles of his face hardening as his thoughts raced.

"Did you tell him we were together?" she asked.

"Not exactly," he admitted. "But he's not stupid."

Her stomach churned. "And he knows you're still in Montreal?"

He rubbed the back of his neck, his movements tense. "I told him I'd go off the radar for a while until things cooled down. I didn't give him specifics."

"Are you going to meet him?" The tremor in her voice betrayed the calm she desperately tried to project.

He stepped closer, his intense gaze softening as he wrapped her in his arms. She melted into him, the warmth of his body a stark contrast to the icy fear clutching at her chest. He pressed a lingering kiss to the crown of her head, breathing her in like she was the only thing tethering him to the moment.

"I'll meet him," he said finally, his voice quiet but resolute. "If Clayton's reaching out like this, it's serious. But I'll handle it."

Seated at the bar of a bistro, Jesse took a slow sip of his beer, his mind a whirl of anxiety. His new identity was supposed to be his shield, his chance to fade into the shadows. But Clayton's unexpected visit had frayed that illusion. Piece by piece, the safety he'd built was coming undone.

"Good to see you, man," Clayton's voice interrupted his spiraling thoughts. The words carried a warmth Jesse hadn't felt in days, a flicker of normalcy in the chaos.

Jesse stood, forcing a casual grin as Clayton pulled him into a brief embrace. "Looking sharp," he added, giving him a once-over, but the approval in his words was tempered by concern.

"The ladies seem to think so," Jesse quipped, forcing a chuckle as he ran a hand through his hair. The remark felt hollow, even to him.

Clayton's expression darkened. He leaned in, his voice dropping low. "I spoke to Hugues and Jay. The police questioned them."

The words hit Jesse like a cold punch to the gut. "What did they ask?"

"About you. Where you've been, who you've been seen with." Clayton's tone grew heavier. "Word is, they know you're at the Tux. And the stuff they seized from Club Viator? They're piecing it together. It's bad."

A shadow passed over Jesse's face, his grip tightening around the glass until his knuckles turned white. "Shit."

"If you stay in Montreal, it's just a matter of time before they catch up with you," Clayton said, his voice softening with something that almost resembled regret. "I know why you don't want to leave. But maybe it's time to ask yourself whether staying is worth the risk."

Jesse exhaled a long, slow breath, his eyes fixed on the amber liquid swirling in his glass. The room around him blurred, the noise of distant chatter fading into the background. For a moment, he was lost—caught between the life he had built and the looming threat of losing it all.

When he finally returned home, the sight that met him made his chest tighten. Talie was lying on the bed, her face buried in the pillow. Her shoulders trembled, and her red, swollen eyes betrayed the tears she had been fighting all night. The stillness in the room was deafening. He hesitated in the doorway, his heart heavy as he tried to summon the words to comfort her, to ease the depth of her pain. But nothing came.

"Is it bad?" Her voice cut through the silence, barely above a whisper.

"It's… complicated," he murmured, sitting down beside her.

"Damn it, Jesse," she cried, her voice trembling with desperation. "What are we going to do?"

He reached for her hand, intertwining his fingers with hers, grounding himself in her touch. "I'll figure it out," he said, the words a promise to her as much as to himself.

She looked up at him, her tear-filled eyes searching his face, searching for the cracks in his armor, for any sign that their world might come crashing down. But Jesse's face remained set with determination.

"What's the plan?" she asked, her voice small, afraid of the answer.

He dropped his gaze to their joined hands, the ghost of Grace's words whispering in his mind: *Even though life is full of challenges, never doubt your inner strength.* A lump formed in his throat, and he had to steady himself. "I just need some time," he whispered, inching closer to her.

Talie's gaze held his, her breath catching at the raw vulnerability shining in his blue eyes. In that moment, she saw it all—the fear, the burden, the overwhelming sadness he carried in silence. It almost shattered her, seeing him like this, the weight of the world etched so deeply into his features. For a fleeting second, it was as if she could feel it too—an ache so deep it threatened to consume them both.

Unable to bear the thought of her witnessing the torment etched into his soul, Jesse closed his eyes and kissed her with a tenderness that spoke of forever. In that kiss, he poured everything—his love, his fears, his hopes—imprinting the memory of her soft lips against his, as if it were the last time they would ever touch.

ABOUT THE AUTHOR

Sabrine Sadler writes stories about **love, friendship, and self-discovery**. Passionate about shopping, travel, and healthy living, she brings vibrant experiences into her books.

Her debut series, **Why Not?**, is a refreshing take on modern relationships, seduction, and the pursuit of happiness. With the upcoming release of **volumes 2 to 5**, she promises readers an unforgettable journey filled with passion, suspense, and life-changing decisions.

www.ingramcontent.com/pod-product-compliance
Lightning Source LLC
LaVergne TN
LVHW050859200726
843508LV00011B/2056